Impish

Ashlyn Grace

Library of Congress Control Number: 2018675309
Printed in the United States of America

For those who love All Hallow's Eve

Contents

~Prologue~

The Veil

October 31, 2002

Julia could hardly contain herself.

As the setting sun shot fire and life across the sky, the little town of Murkwood had turned out in storm to embrace the single most fun and important night of the year: Halloween. Excitement rose, almost as tall as the waving scarecrows that guarded the entrance to the festival like dutiful, silly, stuffed knights in shining armor.

Tugging at her daddy's sleeve she grinned, "Look! Look, Dad, see the moon? It's full tonight. You know what that means, don't you?"

Eric Murphy prided himself on being a simple man. A man who earned his keep, washed behind the ears and did his level best not to take for granted a single shiny moment on God's green Earth. Sure, he'd married himself a witch - and that certainly did tend to color things up a bit - but there was still plenty of good old black and white to be found in this life to his way of thinking. And one of those universal truths, like 'listen to your Mama' or 'don't go poking bears with sticks', was the foundational fact that kids make up the darnedest things.

So when his little girl blinked up at him with those brilliant golden eyes, he could do little else but send her an indulgent smile and listen attentively - even when most everything that came out of her adorable little mouth nowadays was utter bullshit. "What's that, Sweetie?"

Julie's eyes widened, in shock or outrage he wasn't sure, but seven whole years on this planet sure did give her loads of things to teach him apparently.

"The full moon is the most powerful of the moon's phases! And tonight's All Hallows Eve!" Her voice dropped to a reverent whisper, "Do you know what that means?"

Eric shook his head.

"The veil is thin!" She shouted it with none of the spooky reverence of before, "It's *thin!* Imagine the possibilities!"

Eric's brows rose, "Possibilities?"

She shook her head at him like she couldn't believe he was so sad.

"Spells are extra powerful tonight!" She was all but vibrating with excitement, "I could try so many things! I could make myself blond like Angie," She twirled her long dark hair around her finger as she considered, ticking each one off on little fingers laden with her Gran's most glittery costume jewelry, "Or do a call to the elements or even turn Timmy into a frog!"

Oh, that would be a good one. Her eyes sparked with wicked glee at the thought of the nasty little boy that lived down the lane croaking his way to school each morning.

Eric chuckled and ruffled her hair, "I don't know about that now..."

"He deserves it," She pouted.

"Oh, I know." Eric chucked her under the chin, "I meant the blond." He narrowed his eyes and scrunched his nose like he was trying to visualize it until she giggled, "Nope. Nope. Gotta say, you are too darn pretty just the way you are."

She rolled her eyes hugely, "Well of course you think so. You're my dad."

"And the one who's looking at you as it happens. Let's just keep it as is for now, alright?"

Rather than answering, she froze. Her eyes going wide as she stared up at him.

He tugged at her curl a couple times before leaning close and making a show of scanning the little harvest festival, "What is it?" He whispered. It all looked pretty normal to him, kids and parents ambling from booth to booth to play at spooky games and taste spooky things.

"Dad. Oh my gosh..." Little hands slapped to her over-blushed cheeks, "The veil is thin."

"You said that already."

"Yeah, but what about the other side? Who knows what might come through!" Her eyes twinkled as she leaned close once more, "We might even get to meet -" She made a show of looking side to side to make sure no one was listening in, "A goblin!" She practically danced for joy, "An honest to god Goblin, Dad! How cool is that?"

"Pretty cool, I'd say." Her daddy chuckled and reached out to straighten her glossy fairy wings, sending up a brief thanks that she'd gone with Fairy Princess rather than the zombified mermaid she'd been so adamant about weeks prior. What the hell even was a Siren anyway? The things people think up these days...

Before she could launch into another tirade about some godforsaken monster or another, his friend Travis called out from beside the beer garden and Eric lifted his hand in greeting. "Just a minute!" He turned back to his pretty little princess – God, but he didn't know how he'd been blessed with such a sweet little beauty, all curiosity and light just like her mama - and tugged one last stray curl into place. "Run along now, Sweetie. I'm gonna go say hi and rustle up a drink or two."

Immediately her face fell, her lower lip poked out and even her pretty little eyes dimmed.

"Hey, now. What's all this?" Eric poked at her side until she almost broke into a smile.

"But you promised!" She whined, "You said we were going to carve pumpkins and get our faces painted and do the maze-"

"And we will!" He poked her again just for good measure, "I'm just going to be friendly for a minute or two. Why don't you go on and do the same? Look," He nudged her around and pointed towards the corn field where a shabby wooden signpost had been pounded deep into the soil to mark the start of the maze. A small group of ghosties and ghoulies gathered there armed with plastic tubs of candy, swords and light sabers. "There's Hunter now. Why don't you go on and catch us a place in line so we can all go through together."

"But Dad..." She sighed the long-suffering sigh of a seven year old, "Hunter doesn't like me. He says me and Mama and Gran are weird. He called us witches and said how we're evil cuz the Bible says so."

"Oh he did, did he?" Eric lifted a brow and scanned the brooding little Thor next to the corn maze. Sounds like it's about time to have a chat with Travis after all, friendliness aside.

"Yeah."

"Well, the best way to fight a bully is to kill 'em with kindness. He says anything off to you, you just smile and say 'Happy Halloween'. You hear me?"

"But Dad..."

He flicked at her lower lip and nodded the way, "Go on now. Save us a spot. I'll be right along."

Julie heaved another sigh and begrudgingly nodded before moping over to get in line. She sure hoped he didn't take too long cuz she was pretty darn sure that saying nice things to Hunter Thompson wouldn't do much to keep the kid's fat mouth shut.

"What are you supposed to be? Some kind of candy witch that tricks kids into their cabin to eat 'em?" Hunter snickered with his two best friends Brook Headley and Ryan Gregor, and adjusted his viking helmet so he could look down his nose at her.

He was a couple years older than her and boy, did he like to lord it over all the little kids whenever he got the chance. She didn't even know why he thought he was so dang cool – his hair was the color of straw and he always looked sorta sunburned cuz his cheeks were always so red. Sure, he was alright at sports but being okay at hitting a baseball doesn't make you king of the world. Even if your daddy owned lots of the stores and stuff downtown.

"Nu-uh. I'm a Fairy Princess. What are you supposed to be?"

Hunter sniffed, "Thor. Obviously. Jeez, are you never allowed to watch a movie in that hovel?"

Julia crossed her arms and stamped her foot, "It is NOT a hovel." Not that she knew what hovel meant but she was pretty sure it was mean. "Our house is super nice! It's got loads of rooms and gardens and-"

"To keep kids prisoner before you eat 'em, I bet."

"NO!"

"Julia," Her dad's voice held a distinct note of warning and she rolled her eyes again.

"Happy Halloween," She grumbled.

Hunter leaned closer, "What was that? Couldn't hear you."

She gritted her teeth and glared. "Happy Halloween," She sneered.

"Betcha can't wait to get out of all that glitter, since today is the only day you can be all green and warty without anyone calling you on it."

That was it.

Screw Timmy Baskins, she was totally turning *him* into a toad. Totally. A horrid little Hunter toad with nasty little black eyes and a good coating of slime. Green slime. Smelly slime. Slime so slimy even his mom wouldn't let him back in the house.

But tears of frustration pricked and desperation rose right along with them. She couldn't let him see that he got to her - she just couldn't. Her daddy always said that kids bully to get a rise out of you and maybe that was part of it, but right now she just couldn't let him win like that.

Shoving by hard enough to knock Thor right onto his stupid Thor butt, she plunged head first into the maze all by herself. She didn't pause for a second, not until she couldn't hear Hunter's pissed off moaning to his daddy about how mean she was or her own father's exasperated sigh.

Well, she could be exasperated too.

She was tired of it! She'd *told* him and *told* him that Hunter was mean to her, but just because stupid Travis was his stupid friend she had to be nice to his stupid kid. It wasn't fair! With a bad tempered grunt, she shoved corn aside and stomped on through, not caring if she broke it or not.

It was Hunter's fault, far as she was concerned.

She didn't notice the shadows shift and deepen - not at first. It just suited the mood.

She'd worked herself into a good mad now and it felt kinda good. So she kept on muttering, kept on clenching and unclenching her tiny fists around the sparkly star wand that she and her Mama had decorated with *extra* sparkles to make it extra special. The full moon seemed oddly close now, it took up the whole sky and shined silvery over the field - but that was probably just Halloween magic. It was the most magical night of the year after all, and now she couldn't wait to get home and get Gran to help her hex Hunter into oblivion.

She'd make it so he couldn't ever say her name again.

Or 'witch'. That would be even better.

Or, she thought with an evil grin, she'd make it so he could never taste candy again. Any candy. Ever.

Yeah, that would be *perfect*.

Satisfied she'd come up with the perfect revenge, she turned on her heel to head back to her dad. They'd get their faces painted like he'd promised and then she was totally going to show Hunter exactly what a witch could do. She'd even watch as he tried to eat that first piece of candy and it tasted like nothing but dirt and-

Where's the corn?

Everything stalled. Shadows stretched from all directions, reaching toward her like fingers as she stood in the center of a little meadow surrounded by tiny purple wildflowers that just... Shouldn't be there.

She stared at the flowers, nostrils flaring as she tried to work through how it was possible. They were pretty enough but they were freaking her out. Her daddy was a farmer, their land bordered the Gregor Farm just over the far ridge, and she'd tromped these fields more times than she could count when he'd come to help them out here and there throughout the year. And there were two things she knew for certain: there weren't any meadows on the edge of these fields - the corn gave way to onion and then radish before she'd ever hit the tree line - and it was way too cold at night in October for wildflowers.

But it wasn't cold at all.

Something tugged at her – in her tummy, in her soul. She'd felt that kind of energy before, when her Mama or her Gran would practice the Craft with her, but it had never been so direct, or so strong.

There was magic here.

Julia rubbed at the goosebumps on her bare arms and shivered, thinking of the jacket she'd made her daddy leave in the truck cuz she didn't want to ruin her costume. He'd said it was supposed to get cold enough to even frost tonight but it was almost... warm.

It wasn't even night - or it shouldn't be. Not like this anyhow. The sun hadn't even set yet when they'd reached the festival and it couldn't have been more than a few minutes she'd been stomping around. She hadn't been *that* mad... Right? Her round eyes tracked up to the too-close moon and this time she let the tears fall. It was barely dinner time.

The veil is thin.

Holy crap!

"Calm now, Little One."

Julia shrieked and fell on her butt just like Thor had, her sparkly wand falling from numb fingers. The voice was low, soothing. A man's voice - but definitely not her dad, she'd know her dad anywhere and this was too gruff for that. "H-Hello?"

Trees rustled to her side and she squinted at the shadows, they were so deep and black it was hard to tell what she was looking at.

"Hello, Child." The accented voice stayed even, gentle - like how someone talks to a scared dog or horse or something.

It moved and Julia gulped. The man had to be the tallest guy she'd ever seen in her life, and when he crouched slowly she could see something that looked for all the world like those bare reaching branches crouching with him.

No.

When she didn't run he moved a little, shifting just enough that the moonlight glinted off his antlers – honest to god *antlers* - that rose wicked and high from his forehead like a towering crown.

“Are you lost?”

“I-” She stared. She knew it was rude, she just couldn’t help it. “I think so.”

The creature nodded, his horns nodding too. “What is your name?”

She blinked, “I’m not allowed to say.”

“Oh?” His eyes glowed. They actually glowed orange in the darkness like some kind of eerie, laughing lantern. “And why’s that?”

“I’m not supposed to talk to strangers.”

“I see.” He rolled to his butt too so that they both sat on the same soft ground, but she still had to look up to meet his eyes. “That’s a very good rule. Who came up with it?”

“My daddy.” She sucked in a bolstering breath and tried to look fierce and threatening as she stared him down, “And he’s really big and smart and- and mean too! He’s definitely going to hurt you if you try to mess with me!”

The antlers tilted, the eyes glowing so brightly she could almost see him smile, “Just as a father should do, I’d say.” He studied her, his gaze soft and gentle. “Where are you from, Little Princess?”

“I’m not a princess.”

“Well then, you certainly fooled me. Where are you from, Little Fairy?”

Julia chewed on her lip, golden eyes shining with an enticing mixture of nerves and cunning.

Thrynn had never seen anything like her in his life.

Of course, he’d seen Humans before - he’d traveled to Earth many times in his day, countless other worlds too - but never had he seen a soul shine so brightly, so purely as the one that perched before him now. She was like sunshine incarnate, glittering and gold, emitting a warmth and - oddly enough - a comfort that tugged at him to his core.

He wanted her.

It was a strange sensation, one he couldn't recall ever feeling save for family. He wanted to guard her, guide her. See her smile and laugh.

Her giggle would light the wilds, he was certain.

But right now her eyes shone with fear and it twisted his heart. He rolled his shoulders, easing the slight ache that pulsed through the wings hidden beneath his glamour. A soul like hers should never be tainted like that. At least not because of him - not ever.

Considering, a little amused at himself for caring at all, Thrynn gestured to the shadows at his back. "Don't frighten her now," He murmured in his native tongue and the little thing nodded it's understanding with a flick of it's tail. If it were possible, the child's eyes stretched even wider at his words, but he gentled her with a smile.

"Come."

At his side a little creature crawled slowly from the shadows, stubby horns protruding from his tiny angular face as his bulging yellow eyes and stark white fangs glinted in her shine. He looked just as fascinated, his eyes focused on the little fairy princess as she glittered and gleamed, gripping her little wand like a warrior wields his sword. A smile slowly curved his thin lips. His leathery skin was the color of bark, his mane red and wild, curling from his crown and down his spine to cover his legs in thick protective fur. The tufts on his elbows bristled when the child looked on him and gasped, so Thrynn whispered a gentle command.

Immediately the creature shifted, it's visage taking on that of a hare with long flicking ears and soft fur. The colors were all wrong, it's eyes still yellow and it's hair all red and brown, but it's fangs had receded and it looked harmless enough. It's nose wiggled charmingly, it's cotton tail perked at attention as it hopped closer to inspect the frightened little female.

"It's alright. He's friendly," Thrynn murmured, smiling softly at her when the girl's eyes flicked suspiciously up to his.

The bunny hesitantly hopped even closer and nudged her fingers with his nose until she relented enough to scritch at his ears. Then he rumbled and thumped his foot in appreciation.

A hesitant giggle tinkled about the meadow, casting color and light bubbling straight to the stars.

Thrynn sucked in a breath - he *knew.*

His gut clenched, the beast within rumbled because it knew too.

Impossible.

Simply incredible.

This... No. She was a child, captivating and sweet, open and honest, innocent-

And lost.

She had a father, likely a mother and family waiting for her on the other side. People she loved and trusted – a being didn't glow without coming from a light like that.

Mine.

The thought rocked him, the possessiveness deep and instinctive.

But to keep her would be to hurt her... And that was simply unacceptable.

Although it was hard - harder than he'd ever expected - he rose to his feet with a promise, "He'll take you home." Nodding to the hare he waited until the creature met his eyes and nodded solemnly. She would be safe here in this territory. With him.

He had no idea why the thought made him jealous.

Ridiculous. Gritting his teeth on a huff, he headed back to the trees. A run was what he needed. Maybe a flight. Good and hard, until he couldn't think or move or dwell on this insanity another instant-

"Wait!" Julia squeaked, scrambling to her feet too quickly to be graceful about it.

Thrynn's shoulders tightened, he turned back slowly and

lifted a brow.

"I just-" Julia cleared her throat and tried again, "Thank you, Mister."

Though it cost him, Thrynn smirked and sent her a nod, bleeding into the shadows of the trees as he did. "Be safe, Little One..."

'Till we meet again.

~Chapter One~

A Pox on Murkwood

September 20, 2021

Never would a day go by without a visit from her unwelcome friend.

Well, friend was pushing it, but over the years she'd endeavored to seek out any tiny ray of sunshine she could find as she muddled her way through the gator infested swamp nest that was her life. Julia blew out a resigned breath and studied the being floating outside her second story apartment window as she poured her morning coffee and cracked an egg into a skillet for some breakfast.

It had donned the visage of a young Asian boy today – probably something it had picked up spying on her collection of mediocre horror movies – but the color choices were all wrong. It's eyes gleamed crimson and lit with giddy madness every time she met them. It's skin was a sickened slate shade of gray and damp with a sulfer-smelling film of rot that resembled what one would find coating food that's spent too long in the back of your fridge – she could always tell when the little bastard was pissed at her because he left a trail of the crap like some godforsaken slug poking through her pantie drawer. When he grinned like he was doing now his mouth stretched just a little too far and his teeth shone yellow and sharp like a shark. And to top it all off, he was only about the size of a chubby house cat.

Yeah...

When it came to mimicry the little dude was definitely not Class A.

The thing had been a thorn in her side ever since that stupid Halloween festival she'd gone to when she was seven years old. Murkwood, Kansas, witches and pumpkins and cauldrons full of questionable drinks, costumes and spooky stories, and - a personal favorite - the corn maze. Julia had always believed in magic, and there was plenty to be had that night in that crazy-rich town dead in the heart of the heartland. She'd been utterly enthralled by it all, and - because she was a precocious little snot - when she'd been told to wait in line for the guide to bring them through the maze, she'd just barreled right on in.

Worst decision ever.

Sure, she'd been trying to avoid gut-punching little Hunter Thompson for being a phenomenal jerk, but it wasn't her usual M.O to run off on her own like that. For years she'd wondered about it – Why hadn't she just stomped back to her dad? Why hadn't she kicked him in the shin and left it at that? ... In the end all she could figure was that it must've been fate.

She'd felt the draw of the magic that evening. Once the shock had worn off it had tingled beneath her skin, tugging at her spirit like the pied freaking piper. That call had resonated straight down to the bone - she remembered it clearly because it was a feeling she'd devoted a lifetime to recreating. You'd think it was an invitation. Had to be, right? How could something so clear, so tempting, so *right* not be for her?

But nope.

She'd trespassed.

And now she was stuck with slug-boy.

At least that was what she'd surmised from her research these last twenty-odd years.

The creature, she'd dubbed him Little Rude for his absolutely obnoxious timing and his irritating tendency to scare the living bejeezus out of any normal person who dared wander within a five-mile radius of her, was an Imp. A lesser Fae that had glommed onto her when he'd guided her back through the veil all those years ago. Since then, they'd formed a bond of sorts.

An unwilling... Weird... Probably even slightly abusive bond.

But a bond nonetheless.

And, sad as it sounds, apart from her parents and her dear old Gran, it was just about the only relationship she'd managed to keep over the years. She loosed a windy sigh and sipped her coffee. It was hard enough to play the dating game when you were the oddball out in a small town, but add on a little monster that seemed hell-bent on freaking anyone out that dared come to visit, and her love life fizzled and died a sad, somber, lonely death. Same goes with work, and friends for that matter.

It wasn't all bad though. He treated her well enough, and she was fairly sure he'd even gone to bat for her a time or two over the years. Thinking back, it was just after he'd arrived that the bullying had stopped - just stopped like it had never even been a thing - and after it had, it was like the town just unanimously deemed her and her family cool. Strange, odd, eccentric even. But cool. Even the Reverend had started sending them welcoming nods when they ran into each other on the streets, and he'd always had a stick lodged firmly up his butt. She'd never asked Rude if he'd had something to do with that – don't look a gift horse in the mouth and all – but she'd always felt grateful.

Even if his methods tended towards the more... Uncouth.

She was fairly sure that he fed on fear, or at least had this intrinsic drive to negative energy, as he obsessed over all things spooky and gross. No matter what movies they'd watched or pictures she'd shown him, everything from Disney to anime, nothing seemed to float his boat if it wasn't at least a little grotesque.

Even now he slobbered at the window, eyes glinting and nostrils flaring at the scent of the bacon she slipped beside the eggs to fry. Hope and excitement vibrated him enough to shake the damn glass.

"Oh, for eff's sake..." She muttered as she slid an extra couple pieces in beside hers, rolling her eyes as Rude grinned wickedly with delight. "Come on then," She nodded inside but didn't bother to go unlock or open the window - he wouldn't need it anyhow.

A moment later the little creature emerged from the

shadows of the hall, half skipping towards her sofa-

"Hey," Her voice held warning and Rude hesitated, his eyes meeting hers before he seemed to puff out a sigh of his own and grabbed one of the towels she stashed among the blankets in the basket beside the couch. Though he snapped it as he spread it over the cushion, he perched on it carefully enough. "Thank you."

When he sent her an exaggerated roll of his eyes, she only smiled.

For a daemon, he really wasn't all that bad.

While he turned on her television, he muttered in his native tongue - she was mostly sure it was a language anyway, though he'd never bothered to learn hers. She'd spent some time as a child teaching him how to read English, wear clothes or some kind of inoffensive visage, knock and act politely in the hopes of making him into a more normal friend; but the only thing that seemed to stick was the reading. Figures, she scoffed and watched as he searched Netflix for something satisfyingly bloody. It was almost like having a kid brother, funk and all.

With a rueful shake of her head she opened her laptop and scrolled through her orders for the day.

Three healing lotions for eczema.

Two of her more favored charged candle sets.

A number of tea mixtures for sleep, for protection, for prosperity.

And - *Effing Hell* - This guy again. What was it with assholes and hexes anyhow?

As a hereditary witch of the ó Súilleabháin line, Julia Marie Murphy had grown up to all the wondrous stories and tales, tricks and treats of the Old Ways. She loved magic dearly and, though she'd been plenty tempted a time or two to follow through on some of the more creative of her childhood threats, she could proudly proclaim that she had never broken the Craft's most cardinal rule: *An it harm none.* The Law of Three applied to everyone - even those unwilling to acknowledge it - and so, even as a freelance witch-for-hire with bills to pay and Imps to feed, there were certain lines Julia was just unwilling to cross. For safety's sake.

She would boil and brew, cook and charge anything from healing ointments to glamour spells, but she would never dabble in hexes, curses or love spells. You just didn't tramp all over someone's free will like that - Hell, for all she knew this nutter was some psycho-stalker trying to hurt someone who'd kicked his ass to the curb for very valid reasons. She didn't know, so she didn't act.

Still, it was weird. Most people get pissed and stew in a good mad for a while until time and life just naturally cool their jets. Not so with Mr. HxHvd@gmail.com.

It had started with requests for full on curses. He wanted to bend the will, bind the body... Creepy crap that could have - and well would have, had she taken the bait - landed someone in the hospital or dead. Then, when she didn't respond positively to the outright maiming of an individual (justified or not), he had shifted the narrative. Suddenly it had been orders for hexes tailored to an individual - minor things, nuisances. Things like causing the target to suddenly develop an allergy to peanuts or making it so they could never speak his name again. But she'd continued to refuse. After all, this guy hadn't given her any reason to believe he was acting in self defense – a nut allergy? Seriously? What kind of attack could you be circumventing with that?

Eventually it had morphed into questions about the Craft, her traditions and her power, her capabilities. Normally, she didn't have an issue sharing that kind of thing with her clientele, it was only good business to contribute encouragement and good old fashioned know-how to the blossoming New-Age community, but his questions had been pointed and even invasive. Like he was taunting her, learning her, doing his best to provoke her into acting on his behalf.

That was probably ridiculous paranoia, but still...

She'd avoided most of it, calmly explaining her reasoning and the Law of Three. Everything you put out into the Universe will roll back to you times three. So if you live your life well, if your intent remains clear and kind, then that kindness will come right on back around when you need it. Same goes for the nasty crap. Karma was a very real thing so she did her best to steer him towards a lighter path without overly involving herself. There are always many ways to achieve a goal after all, and the best revenge is living well. *Kill 'em with kindness*, her daddy always said.

Nothing had stuck, evidently.

Muttering to herself, she trashed the latest set of questioning and saved breakfast moments before it was burned beyond repair. Then nearly jumped out of her skin when she turned around to find Rude hovering all but nose to nose with her, "Rude!" She shoved his little shoulders away, "Cripes, Dude, it's enough to give me a freaking heart attack!"

When he grinned she jabbed a finger at him, "And then who would cook your damn eggs?"

His face fell.

"That's what I thought." She nodded back to the sofa, "Now go sit down and I'll bring you your plate." When he yipped excitedly and snapped his teeth in her direction she shooed him off, "And quit with that nastiness, I know you don't slime all the freaking time. Cool it."

He lifted a considering brow.

"I mean it, Rude. Don't make me eat your bacon in front of you. I will."

His eyes narrowed.

She clutched her stomach, "Oh-so-*hungry!* And look! I have all this tasty bacon to-"

She snickered when his eyes widened and he poofed back to the sofa, hands folded in his lap and spine straight enough to make even the snootiest Mary Poppins proud.

Shaking her head, she piled their plates high with eggs and bacon, poured them each a glass of water and hauled everything over to where Rude perched. *Waiting on a daemon*, she sighed and rubbed at the back of her neck. So this was the glamorous life of a cottage witch, eh? No wonder people ditched the tradition.

That and the ridiculous stereotypes.

While she did live in the Bible belt here in sunny Murkwood, Kansas, she was lucky enough to have a hometown that seemed to truly give a damn about it's families, colorful or plain as the driven snow. So although some of the more fundamentalist Churchies tended to glare or cross themselves at the sight of her, she had carved out a happy little niche regardless.

And she *was* a witch - so she couldn't really blame them, after all. *Thou shalt not suffer a witch to live,* and all that jazz.

Rude made happy little smacking sounds as he tucked into his breakfast and watched avidly as a giant Megalodon menaced an unsuspecting coastal town. Julia sighed, already the little Imp's teeth were sharpening into little serrated triangles like tiny terrible copies of the shark's on screen. At least this was an underwater monster - she was far less likely to wake up in the middle of the night to an unpleasant surprise. Gods, she shuddered remembering the mess he'd made after he saw *The Ring* for the first time, water and filth all over the living room, and she'd had to replace two television sets before he finally found something else to fan boy.

"Welp," She slapped her thighs and rose with a stretch and an exaggerated yawn, "Better get to it, I guess."

Rude didn't bother to look at her.

She planted herself in front of him and scratched her stomach, "You know what I could use? A helper. A little one about three, maybe four feet tall... Two hands, two feet. Know anyone like that?"

Rude rolled his eyes up to her face and poofed into an ugly, wiry black dog.

"Nice."

He just settled his head on his paws, panting and staring at the screen when she moved on.

Julia just rolled her eyes. Typical. Apart from jumping in from time to time to remind her not to burn their dinner, Rude was utterly useless. Well, that wasn't entirely fair. She half-suspected the magical boost she'd seen in her Craft was due to him – at least in part. The little dude didn't strike her as the most competent user, creature of the Otherworld or not.

Because the weather seemed to call for it with it's long, lazy summer days, she lazed her way through her routine, sporting a pair of distressed jean shorts she'd had since high school and a t-shirt that had, at some point, been black. It was roomy though, and that was nice because it was about a billion and one degrees outside and today she had to venture forth on a noble quest to the local nursery. Her fire-escape garden and her window boxes served her well enough most days but sometimes it just couldn't keep up with whatever the trending need happened to be.

"I'm off," She called to Rude as she collected her bag from the counter and twisted her hair haphazardly into a clip. "Don't wreck the place, you hear me?"

Dog-Rude snuffed in her direction.

"Good enough," She muttered and headed out.

Her apartment building sat smack dab in the center of her picturesque little town filled with picturesque places and people. Not that they were always pretty, mind, but they were interesting and kind enough most days to make up for the lack of shine. These were good, honest folk doing their best in the way they knew how, and she loved them for it. Even now as she ambled down the street to Andrea's Garden, people paused to wave at her, to ask after her family, herself.

It was a lovely thing, she figured, to feel like the whole of a place was your home.

"Hey now, Witchy-Woo, how are you?"

Julia chuckled and sent Old Man Gregor a wink. He'd probably once been a fairly formidable dude, but years of hard labor and raising four 'strapping young lads' as he liked to say had curved his spine until he was about face to face with her. Not that the bend in his spine in any way indicated a bend in his spirit. Not even a little bit. Even now he stood, shaking his carved walking stick up at the Thompson carpentry crew and shouting over the booms and bangs of building. Hunter Thompson himself had even bothered to come on down from his perch on the roof framing to see what all the fuss was about, and he looked so darn flustered Julia couldn't help but wander over to poke her nose in.

"How's it going, Handsome?" She gave the old man a squeeze.

"Handsome?" He cackled and scratched his belly. When he grinned the gaps in his teeth were large enough to toss a penny through, and his wrinkles piled so high on his cheeks his eyes got lost in them. "Ain't so sure about that. But I'll tell you one thing: It'll be rain tonight, that's for certain."

Hunter rolled his eyes to her and mouthed *save me.*

Julia squinted up at the cloudless sky, "Oh yeah?"

"We needs it too. Corns all but hacking, how little we've got this year. Strange, strange times, I'll say."

Julia lifted her brow, "It rained last Tuesday."

"Bah," Gregor spat and then mumbled an apology for doing such a thing in front of a lady. "Barely. But it'll be a good one tonight. You just wait and see." He poked Hunter in the chest, "I'm telling you, Boy. You'd do well to put everything under cover this evening, that's all."

"Ain't nothing in the news says anything about rain," He scowled and rubbed at the spot he'd been jabbed. Even as a grown man, Hunter couldn't help but be contrary. Hoping for some camaraderie he looked to Julia who just crossed her arms, smirked and lifted a brow. "Not that I don't appreciate the concern," He mumbled.

Julia sniffed and relented enough to send him a full on smile. For a spoiled brat, Hunter had actually made something pretty decent of himself over the years. He'd never lost that ever-blush or the straw colored hair, but he'd figured out a way to tame it all into something relatively appealing, and by high school he'd been leading the football team to victory two years running. Now he owned his own carpentry company and did decent work if the rumors were to be believed.

"I've been working this land, under this sky for sixty-damn-years. Ain't no fancy weather man goin' tell you truer than that."

"Hm..." He had a point. Who was she to argue? The weather had warned of unprecedented high temperatures for the coming week but when it came to choosing between a barometer and Old Man Gregor? Old Man Gregor won every time. "I'll be sure to pull my herbs in, then."

"See?" He hollered up at Hunter who just loosed an exasperated sigh. "You do that, Sweetie. And send a hello to your Gran for me, will ya?"

Julia smirked, "She still fighting you?"

The moment he sensed an out Hunter sent her a grateful wave and disappeared back to work.

Gregor narrowed his eyes but let the boy go. Wasn't more he could do anyway, to his thinking. And besides, what man wouldn't give all his attention to such a pretty girl on a pretty day. Hamming it up, he heaved a heavy sigh and tried for beleaguered which won him Julie's charming giggle.

He'd been sweet on her Gran for years but had never managed to finagle a date. Not for lack of trying, "She's a stubborn one, but I've tricks yet."

She chuckled and gave him a quick hug that had the color flooding his cheeks, "I'm rooting for you."

"You tell her so then," Hooking her arm through his with a friendly pat, he led her to the nursery. "What's it to be today then, eh? Something pretty for your porch or another round of herbs for those teas of yours?"

"Business before pleasure, I'm afraid." She scanned him top to bottom, "And how's the blend I made working for you? Have you followed the regimen I suggested?"

"Haven't slept so peacefully in years," He slapped his bad hip, none to gently. "Don't know how ya managed it, but I'm glad of it."

"Just let me know when you need some more, alright?"

He scanned the pretty window box overflowing with a riot of roses and marigolds and daisies speculatively, “What do you think, should I send a bushel on to your Gran?”

“Probably won't win you dinner but it'd make her day, that's for sure.”

“Well, that's good enough for me.”

~Chapter Two~

Stormy Seas

The day passed quickly in orders and calls, and by the time she surfaced to scrounge up some dinner dark rain clouds had begun to form outside the windows.

"Gotta hand it to the man," She muttered as she pulled out the little canopy she'd jury-rigged over her garden years ago to buffer her plants from the majority of the rain.

Rude blinked one eye at a time from his perch on the sill and cocked his head - feline this time but scaly, like some kind of black and green cross between a swamp monster and a kitten.

All the better for running in the storm, she supposed, as was his habit. She was never sure what he did exactly, but whenever the sky began to turn, off he would scamper into the chaos. Which meant that, at least for a few hours, she would finally score some time alone.

The thought would have been far more thrilling if she had someone cute to booty-call but alas, none would be so lucky. Her last playmate had lasted about two months before Rude had finally caught him in the shower - naked and afraid was only fun on TV apparently. Who knew?

Rude blinked at her in that weird one-two way again before leaping from the sill and picking his way down to some bushes at the base of her building.

"No worries, I won't wait up," She muttered but he was already long gone.

Energy pricked her skin the way it does when lightening charged the air - she could taste it. It was strength she could use, a boon from Mother Nature herself, but she was beyond ready to be done with the day. Laziness warred with responsibility, the couch beckoned so sweetly, but that little sense within her – the one her father had deemed 'witchy' years ago – whispered of all the cool stuff she could do with an elemental charge like that. The seasons were changing, the Wheel of the Year turning, and the closer they got to Samhain, the thinner the veil would become. The possibilities were endless and enticing, so she rushed through setting up her stones and candles to catch all they could.

Wiping dirty palms off on her shorts, she stood with a happy sigh. She loved storms. Everything about them. They were excellent little reminders that there was a world beyond her lists and orders, and it was wicked and cool and really freaking gorgeous. And dangerous. The thrill was more than a little addicting – though perhaps a little of that was Rude rubbing off on her.

Heading in to shower and change, she toed aside the little nest he'd made in her closet and picked through her stuff until she found an oversize t-shirt sporting her KU alma mater and about a dozen tiny holes. She wasn't sure why Rude had picked there of all places to set up his bed, but he'd done it since she was a kid. Even after her father had built him his own little dog house complete with a shiny red door for privacy, he'd always preferred a fluffy dog bed tucked just under her clean clothes. He'd even decorated the place, surrounding his spot with odds and ends he's collected and hoarded like a crow throughout his travels. His little dragon's hoard didn't bother her all that much, as long as he doesn't slime it up or bring back anything living or dead.

That was a rule she'd made very, very clear after a very, very nasty surprise when she'd been trying to vacuum not long after she'd moved to this apartment - she shuddered recalling the nasty collection of dead spiders he'd hidden in a jar back there like some kind of trophy. Ugh...

It would have been nice to throw on something silky and sexy, light some candles, pop open some wine and release some tension, but... Oh well, she blew out a sigh. It's not like she owned anything silky and sexy anyway. For the most part her love life had been depressingly a-romantic. But a girl could dream, and - pulling on her ratty sleep shirt and padding out to the living room to light a few candles, pour a glass of wine and flip on a decent movie - she figured two out of three ain't bad.

It wasn't long before the rain began. The rhythm of it lulled her, beating back the gentle aches and pains a good hard day's work brought with it as she curled up under the fluffy chunk-knit blanket her Mama had made for her. The flames flickered and swayed in the wind, the air scented lightly with lavender for relaxation and jasmine for luck. It was soft and sweet, like the romance she'd thrown on, and she burrowed deep into the cushions to bask.

Her eyes were heavy, but that was alright. Her breathing gentle and even. Thunder rumbled and lightening snapped across the sky as her wet hair curled down her back... *swaying gently in the breeze as the storm ignited a fire at her core.*

She reveled in it.

Her head rolled back, chest open and arms outstretched to the sky. The cliffs were wild tonight, standing mighty against the roaring wind, the thrashing sea. Sea salt and static lit the air, whipping her white gown taught to her body until the silk stroked her skin like a lover.

She could taste him.

Rich as whiskey and just as intoxicating. Earthy and feral, an element and a man all wrapped into one delicious package. He was power - terrible power - unlike anything she'd ever encountered in this life or any other. Like a god deigned to walk among man, sipping of the mortal-wine before he'd fly to bring his grace and beauty home to the heavens.

Curiosity.

It was there. Evident in the way his fingers skimmed and gripped, the way his lips teased and tasted, savoring her.

"Beauty..." His voice rode the wind like he owned it.

"You are," She gasped when his teeth grazed her throat in

response. The thrill zipped straight to her core, she couldn't prevent the moan but the wind whipped it away.

"Such light," His breath was just as heady as his taste as he nuzzled her, his jaw rough with stubble. "Such vibrancy."

"What-"

He stole her words with teeth and tongue, dominating her, beating her into a sweaty, lovely submission. Gods, but she wanted to trust him. A longing unlike anything she'd ever known gripped her, urging her to give in, to give him everything.

To kneel.

She wanted to fuck him. She wanted to worship him. She wanted to love him. Trace her tongue over every peak and valley, run her hands through his hair and stare into his eyes as she-

His eyes.

What color were his eyes?

Blinking her own open for the first time, she drew in a gasping breath. Sweet baby Jesus... She screamed as she toppled onto her ass, scrambling away from the edge as fast as she could go – the roiling sea roaring it's fury as it churned hundreds of feet below. Sharp stones gripped at her silken gown, completely see-through now that the white was dripping with wet. They tore at her bare feet as she fought to stand, panic dousing the fire in her core. The man was gone. Nowhere to be found. Yet she could feel him everywhere, on her skin, on her lips - she felt his energy lingering nearby like a promise.

And still she felt the yearning.

"Calm, Sweet Beauty. You are safe."

She didn't feel safe. The storm swirled and morphed, black clouds rolling over and into one another as savage as the sea. Lightening flashed violet. Too low. Too close.

For an instant, everything, everywhere was violet.

"Come."

She screamed as the orgasm ripped her apart, too brutal to be good, as raging as the sky. Falling to her knees, the pleasure quaked through her, vibrating down to her bones as she shuddered under the onslaught. "Gods..." She whimpered.

"Yes." It whispered, the scent riding the wind with the words,

"Gorgeous. Give me more."

Though nothing was there, she felt his arms steady her as his tongue trailed hot and wet up the column of her throat, teeth pressed to skin. "Again."

She cried out. This was just as brutal, just as hot. How could something so hot feel so cold?

"Yes." Stronger now, toying with her.

Something was wrong. Terribly wrong.

"Give me your pleasure. Let go. Let go and let me in."

The yearning was there.

The curiosity.

But Julia said, "No."

There was a beat - everything stilled.

"Then you shall die with the rest of them."

His hands shoved her spine and she careened forward, lifted by wind and rain until she was tossed head first into the dark, hungry sea.

Julia woke with a gasp. Choking. Fuck! She was choking as she rolled from the couch to her knees to vomit water all over the floor. There was nothing but salt and pain, everything ached, but the presence - the man - it was gone.

After a time she rolled to her ass, leaning heavily against her couch. She'd sweat through her KU shirt, it clung to her like a second skin and her hands shook with the remnants of panic. She'd never dreamed like that before. Of course she'd had the occasional nightmare - What kid wouldn't after seeing Friday the 13th for the first time? - but nothing that lingered. Nothing that felt so... Visceral.

She felt violated. Exposed.

Scrubbing her hands down her face, she forced herself to get up. Carefully. One step at a time. Jumping at every creak and shadow, she gathered her crap and cleaned up her mess. The pretty candles still flickered on the table, the blanket reeked of sweat and bile. Her hands trembled but she got it done, forcing herself to breathe evenly as she rushed to the shower to scrub.

Off.

She wanted it *off.*

She ripped at her clothes, easing a tad the instant the briny scent hit the floor.

She could still feel him, taste him – and it chilled her to the core. Exhaustion hit but instinct and no little desperation had her reaching in the dark to loose the scalding stream, shivering and freezing despite it all.

Rude wasn't home yet.

Cripes, she fumbled for the switch on the wall.

The lights flickered on - insultingly bright.

And blood trickled from three long gashes wrapping her from spine to breast.

~Chapter Three~

Family Matters

With a back sault and a flourish, Rude flipped onto the fire escape to bare his fangs in Julia's direction. She blinked blearily and managed a half-hearted nod of greeting before she did her best to drown herself in scalding hot coffee. Thank the gods for automatic coffee makers, because mornings and her? They weren't on speaking terms.

Especially today.

When she didn't do anything more to acknowledge him, Rude carefully picked his way through her garden to press his snout to the glass. His form had shifted again. Rather than the swamp-cat thing he had going on last night, he looked like a miniature dragon today - the Hungarian Horntail - ripped off straight from Harry Potter, with the crown of spikes and little puffs of smoke rising from his nostrils and everything. They'd always been fans.

It was almost enough to make her smile.

Almost.

Suddenly chilled, she threw on the soft black cardigan her Gran had knitted for her this past Christmas. It smelled of her, her bright yellow magic had always reminded Julia of daffodils in spring, and she tucked into the memories and the love woven there for comfort.

Still, everything felt too close - too exposed. Even covered in layers of cloth and bathed in the warmth of the morning sun, she felt *seen.* It made her feel silly - it hadn't been real, at least not *really* real - but she couldn't even bring herself to look at the couch. Not yet.

Not when she still felt so… Raw.

Pouring herself another mug of steaming coffee she whipped around to go join Rude on the balcony. Her plants always comforted her, their energy soft, their fragrance chasing the stench of sweat from the air. There was the added bonus of not sharing a room with that freaking couch as well. The chill of autumn helped almost as much as the coffee, and the sway of changing leaves in the wind painted Murkwood in a lovely homage to the Great Cycle.

It was easy, instinctive even, to pulse her power into the air in a gentle call to the elements. As the breeze whipped around to kiss her cheeks and toy with her hair, she felt better. Stronger. Ready to face the demons of the day and…. Hell... Last night as well.

Rude nudged her hand, concerned. When she poked his nose, he nipped playfully at her fingertips. She sighed, "I'm alright." And she was.

Sorta.

Her side felt tight and swollen, the cuts deep enough that she'd probably need stitches if she didn't want the flesh to scar. It was the worst of it by far, but the rest of her ached too. She felt like she'd been mauled by a freaking rabid possum or something. Her arms and legs ached when she moved, bruises marred her knees as though she actually had been thrown to the stones the night before. Raw scrapes burned slightly against the warmth of the mug and, if she closed her eyes, she still felt chilled to the bone like the icy waves of that violent sea still held some small part of her captive. But mostly?

Mostly she felt… Unsettled.

That was a tame word for it but it would do. Prophetic dreams were not her specialty as her gifts didn't tend toward the Sight, and as far as she knew she'd never astral projected accidentally before. She routinely cleansed her home and the whole of the apartment building in order to keep her practice pure, so the idea that this could be a poltergeist of some kind was unlikely. A remnant? A call? This wasn't her area of expertise - but one thing was damn sure: that was no ordinary dream.

That was no bit of raw beef or poorly digested mustard. It wasn't a problem her subconscious was working through or some creative left over from some bad horror movie. It had been directed. Intentional. Like a message or...

An attack.

"Time to call in the troops, I think," She murmured to Rude who puffed smoke in response. "Yeah?" She smirked, "I'm sure they missed you too."

With that she headed inside to pull herself together and call her mom.

Two hours later her Gran burst through the door like a firework, "Jules? Where's my Jules?" In a swirl of color and over sized bags which she promptly dumped right on Rude's head where he napped on the couch, Lillian ó Súilleabháin was a four-foot-nine powerhouse. She cackled at him when the Imp shot up to grumble at her, and the lilt of the Emerald Isles rode her tongue strong as it always had as she called over her shoulder, "JoAnna, you just go put on some tea. Chamomile for calm, I think. And peppermint."

No matter how bad she felt, her Gran had always made her smile. Already her energy was pouring into her space, calming and comforting her. "For?" Julia stood from her desk and rolled the tension from her shoulders. When Rude hopped up to prowl the back of her couch, she ran a careful hand along his horny shoulder to soothe his ruffles.

"Me. I'm wanting the zip."

If the legends were true she'd been a hellion in her early days, terrorizing her little home village of Ardmore, Ireland until Patrick Callahan had managed to tame the beast with a twinkling love of mischief and a dozen roses each week. He'd been a strapping young man and a good husband - the great love of her life, she says. So when he'd passed in the war leaving her and her little girl behind, she'd donned the mantle of grieving widow at the ripe old age of twenty-three and never looked at another man again.

Sorry, Gregor.

She'd taken on her old name and all the weight of the Old Ways with it, devoting herself to becoming the strongest witch and mother she could be. If Julia had learned anything from her over the years, it was how to roll with the punches. Because, as she always said, *Life will fuck you up one side and then the other, but it'll warm you too. There's magic in all of that. It's up to you to figure out how to use it.*

Gran tugged at her collar until Julia obediently bent down so she could cup her cheeks in warm hands and gaze deeply into her eyes. "Didn't sleep a wink last night, did you."

"At least a wink... I think. I called you about a dream, remember?"

She pinched her cheek, "Smart ass."

On a chuckle Julia gave her a real hug before heading over to give her mom the same. "Hey, Mama."

Where Gran was all popping energy and color, JoAnna was calm and sweetly soft. It had always baffled her how they could be so opposite and yet function as perfectly together as a well-oiled machine. They'd always been a unit, even when JoAnna and her dad had married - those jokes about how you not only marry someone, you marry their mother? For the ó Súilleabháin's that was very literally true. Lucky for them, Eric had been steady as a rock and stubborn as a bull. He lead with his heart and when you got a piece of him? You got the whole of him for life - crazy mother in laws, Imps, witches and all.

Not that it was surprising. Her mama was an easy woman to love, her heart just as devoted. Beautiful too, like a fairy queen of lore had somehow wound up stuck in the modern age. Her long golden hair tumbled down her spine and glittered with the crystals she'd always enjoyed weaving into the strands. They were amethyst today, matching the strand at her throat and her ears, adding the perfect hint of glamour to her soft brown cardigan, simple white tee and blue jeans. When she held her, Julia felt her magic embrace her as well, all lavender in sight and scent.

"Not yet," She murmured and pulled away. Her mother's eyes returned to their typical wild gold, the only coloring Julia had inherited from both these women. "At least settle in first, okay?"

JoAnna raised a knowing brow. Julia's gift may not have tended towards the Sight but hers most definitely did. She was an Empath, gifted with the *dàrna sealladh* and the ability to heal. The moment she'd entered her daughter's home, she'd felt it.

A... Darkness.

Something threatening lingered here, it had touched her little girl. Marked her. Deeply.

"You're hurt."

"Tea first, Ma."

JoAnna rolled her eyes but swept into the kitchen, "And what of Rude?"

The moment he heard his name, the Imp perked up to proudly prance over to show himself off to her mom. He'd always had a bit of a crush on her, Julia thought. He'd never done anything to try to scare her or gross her out, even when she'd first brought him home. Mostly he just tried to be around her, pressing himself into her legs like a cat starved of attention.

The brat.

JoAnna chuckled and bent to nuzzle him despite the porcupine thing he had going on right now, "Oh, the Horntail! That's one of my favorites."

Rude preened.

"It looks like you got it just right too! Well done." She slipped him something that looked suspiciously like a piece of chocolate and Rude munched it up with all the class of a rabid dog. JoAnna just giggled as shiny, razor sharp teeth snapped two inches from her face.

The kettle whistled and Julia went to pour the tea, but when her side protested, an irritated sigh puffed from her lips.

"I've got it, Baby. You sit."

JoAnna gently shoved her to the table and just like that,

the women smoothly assumed control of her home. On another day it may have irritated her, but right now Julia gratefully flopped into a seat, rubbing the ache behind her temples away. She would have jumped when small hands landed on her shoulders but she almost instantly relaxed as her Gran chased off the lingering remnants of her headache.

"Got you good, didn't he?"

Julia just grunted, grabbing a cup of tea from the pretty tray her mother had managed to throw together for them.

When she sat, her mama reached out to push some wayward strands of hair behind her ear, "Will you show us?"

Julia flushed, "It was- Well," clearing her throat she pushed through it. It wasn't *her* sexy dream and sugar coating this kind of thing was dangerous. No matter how embarrassing it might be. "Yeah."

It was easier - still unpleasant - but when the women joined hands and cast back to the night before, Julia found it much easier to show them rather than try to explain. The images played out in their mind's eye – distant, removed, like a movie - but Julia still couldn't help but cringe at the man's touch, the painful pleasure, the need. Even now she felt echoes of it, almost like an obsession rooting itself in the back of her skull. Her palms started to sweat, heat curled to her core and although she knew - consciously she knew - that she didn't want it, that it had *hurt,* she couldn't help the tiny part of her that almost yearned to trust the stranger. To submit. Julia showed them it all, they rode her consciousness as the male tongued and teased her, as it took what she hadn't chosen to give. And through it, they didn't speak or move except to squeeze her hands gently in comfort or camaraderie.

Then her Gran gasped, "Jesus, Mary and Joeseph!" Breaking the circle she leaned over and ripped Julia's top up. Both women sucked in startled breaths at the sight of the angry, torn flesh. "Did you do nothing to treat it?"

Julia rolled her eyes, "I was a little preoccupied-"

"There's a darkness here," JoAnna's eyes locked onto her

wound, gleaming a bright gold with her power, "A tether."

Gran's face soured even more if it were possible, "To the wound?"

That would suck. Blood was the strongest source of someone's essence - it was intensely personal and a very quick and effective way to root a spell. And spells that infused the blood? They were damn near impossible to cleanse completely.

But her mom just tilted her head, her eyes still unfocused. "I... Don't believe so. There's something-" She hummed, "It's almost too subtle to see. Like a shield? It's woven within her aura but it's not... The tether is different."

"Where is it?" Gran's own eyes began to glow gold with her magic as she lifted her hands. As her granddaughter's did, her gifts tended to lay more in the practical magics but she could still heal to some degree. "I'll break it."

JoAnna came to her knees beside Julia, pressing her hands over the wound in her side but Julia shoved her away, "No. Not until it's cleansed. We can't risk it transferring to you."

Her mother's brow creased with concern though her eyes remained gone, "But this tether - it's strong, indirect. If you don't let me in, it will hurt you."

Julia gritted her teeth, "Then it hurts." There was no way she was letting anything about this jerkface near her family.

No freaking way.

Gran thumped her on the back, "Atta girl," She murmured. She shoved a wooden spoon in front of her face, "Bite down now. No need to disturb your neighbors."

"No need to sound so cheerful about it," Julia muttered.

Her Gran just smirked, the thrill of active magic lighting her spirit up like Christmas, "Better to get it over with, isn't it? Now come." She unceremoniously shoved the spoon between her teeth when Julia opened her mouth to sass.

Julia scoffed and gripped the arm rests of her chair, fighting through the fear. She needed to calm herself and ground her energy so that she didn't accidentally lash out. The moment she'd managed it, both women pressed their hands to her skin and pain, brutal and burning, engulfed her.

It was as though acid dripped over her entire body, eating it's way through muscle and sinew all the way to her soul. She felt it, curling slowly from their fingers as her family's magic burned yellow and purple. Wood cracked between her teeth. Her heart raced. There was no distraction - no focus. For a time - a minute or an hour, she couldn't know - she lost everything it meant to be Human. Sweat slicked her skin, but the wet did nothing to ease the fire.

This was worse, so much worse, than anything the dream had done. But-

For an instant she felt it - her eyes ripped open through the tears to see - it was orange -

And then it was gone.

As suddenly as the pain began it stopped. There was no dripping this time, just an immediate, intoxicating coolness like aloe vera smoothed over a sunburn. She felt shredded, hollow...

But clean.

"Done," Her Gran pressed a shaking kiss to her forehead, "Brave Girl. Good job." She squeezed her, "Good job."

Her mother cradled her head to her breast but Julia could feel the wet from her tears on her hair. "We need to cleanse the house. It's gone from her but it lingers here."

Gran nodded as Julia shoved up to sitting, trembling and exhausted, "I've got it. You get that wound taken care of."

JoAnna chewed on her lip - it was a habit Julia had inherited. "I don't-"

Julia gripped her hand, "It's alright."

JoAnna tenderly wiped the sweat from her brow, "I can't take it away entirely. The cleansing took too much of your energy, you need to rest."

She nodded.

"This won't hurt," Her mama whispered it even though they both already knew. Julia couldn't remember how many times throughout her life her mother had needed to heal her, calling the wounds into herself to ease her baby girl.

When the mirror image of the slashes stained her mother's white shirt with blood, Julia sucked in a breath, "Wait."

"It's okay."

Warmth infused her - pulsed once, twice, three times - before it eased away. The wounds were still there but the anger was gone, the sensitivity and the throbbing within her mother now.

"Mama-"

But JoAnna just smiled and chucked her chin, "It'll be gone in just a few minutes now, you know that."

She did. But she still hated it. She'd always hated it when her mother took her pain into herself.

Things calmed after that. Her Gran hustled her over to the couch and insisted Rude curl up to guard her. Rude seemed happy enough to be given a job, especially when it was to do nothing but lounge around and watch the other witches do their thing. They worked together, twining their energy with hers to bolster and repair her wards, her circles, her workspace. Then they babied her, snuggling her under warm blankets and drowning her in tea. Hours passed while the women just enjoyed one another, and while her family hovered nearby to wait and see if that darkness would try to come back.

It didn't.

When they finally left and the sun began to set, Julia climbed out onto her fire escape to watch them go, vibrant color and love beneath a painted sky. Perhaps it was because her home felt fresh and clean, or maybe it was because she'd been recharged with their love and tenderness, but Julia sensed it this time. It waited and watched, frustrated and... Curious.

She wasn't sure what drew her eyes, the sun set was gorgeous and comforting, but something else claimed her attention. Something moved. Down in the shadows across the street, in a narrow alley, something violet flashed like fire for just an instant. It scared her - she wasn't sure why - but she gritted her teeth and lifted her chin, standing her ground.

And a soft masculine chuckle whispered on the wind.

~Chapter Four~

Into the Otherworld

Fresh clean air filled his lungs and Thrynn sucked it deep, relieved to finally be home. The Otherworld balanced on the brink of Summer and Fall this eve, it's beauty unparalleled by any realm he'd wandered across in all his years of travel. Creatures and spirits sang their love of the land as they toiled and flirted, pranced and preened. And as he passed, weary and worn from his most recent journey, the forest came alive to welcome him.

Sunlight cast chaotic shadows as he made his way through the undergrowth, but this was his territory, his home, and what darkness encroached posed no threat to him. To ensure it, he cast his essence into the soil, North to the mountain rise, West to the meadows, East to the sea and South to the edge of his claim. As he walked, he probed, working his wards to full strength and reassuring himself that no unwelcome soul had wandered through. Though this land was his by right, birthright and by service, the Usurper refused to acknowledge his claim and had proved numerous times over that his greed outweighed any sense of honor or respect he may have held for the Old Ways. So Thrynn searched – each day, each passing – he cast his energy to the brink of his ability just to reassure himself that neither the false king nor his army of Shades had trespassed in his absence.

Adjusting his burden to rest over his other aching shoulder, Thrynn smiled. He was eager to rest after such a trek, and more than ready for a good, hearty, hot meal. Nothing had come, apart from a few wandering Shades that wandered mindlessly until such time as their master called on them again, and with his barriers reinforced and the creatures singing and bickering all around him, he finally allowed himself to head back. There it stood as it always had -

Yvelta - the main House of his kin and clan.

The trunk of the tree spanned acres, sprawling roots and vines in every direction and shooting high to tower above the cloud line. Pressing his palm to the bark, he let his energy flow deep into the wood, reveling in the warmth of it's recognition even as the runes and crest of his kin lit orange with his power. With a mighty creak - it made him wince, but there would be time to see to such things later - the wood split to welcome him home.

There was a time this House had been home to countless beings, family, servants, honored guests and business partners alike. Thrynn remembered running these halls with the children, laughter and teasing ringing off polished stone like the tinkling of bells. It had smelled different then, lush with his mother's fragrance and the mouth-watering scents of cooking food rather than the cold, damp, musk that lingered now.

It was too much for him, really. It would have been too much for anyone, even had they devoted each day of their lives to it's care. This was a den meant for family, community - but now it was only him.

Well, him and a few useless Imps.

Hopefully his most recent spoils would be able to help with that. Heading to the Western Wing where he kept his chambers, his soft leather boots echoed in the silent halls. When he pushed inside, it was like night and day.

The hearth burned heartily, casting heat and dancing light on walls decorated with art and trinkets, memories of his origins and his travels. Two Imps lounged on his rich velvet cushions, but the moment they saw him they leaped to their feet, bowing deeply before backing into the shadows to wander elsewhere. That was fine. He wasn't in the mood for company just now anyway. They'd left their cook pot over the flame though, and the scent of stew had his fangs lengthening in appreciation.

Perhaps not totally useless, after all.

Though he longed to do nothing more than flop down on those cushions himself to rest and eat in peace, he heaved a sigh and hauled his new treasure to the library.

This would be the next room to restore.

Here lay his family's most prized of all treasures. Tome after tome lined the walls with history and culture, legend and lore. The chamber lay near the heart of Yvelta and reached up their home-tree nearly from root to tip. As a child, his father had kept a staff of ten to see to it's care and upkeep alone but decades had come and gone, and the library had withered with neglect. It was depressingly dank, water and dust had taken their toll, but he hoped to salvage and replace all that he could.

Finally bringing his satchel to his feet, Thrynn reached inside and drew out the thing he'd spelled for travel. Balancing it on it's four feet, he stepped back before whispering his will to the wind and watching as the contraption grew back to it's original size.

A clever device.

Technology such as this was not native to the Otherworld itself, but he'd seen much of it in neighboring realms and he'd always found it fascinating. It stood about the height of an average female of his kind, the top of it's dome hovering just about level with his chest. This one had been fashioned to look similar to it's creators, rounded and stumpy like a boggart but with four arms and four spindly legs instead of two. It's carapace was starkly white and shone like water but it was hard to the touch and sounded almost hollow when he tapped it.

"Initiate."

Red and blue lights blinked to life within the thing, and it stood to stretch it's legs before it settled with a series of staccato sounds that rose at the end like a question.

"Language select, Vrykterian." It wasn't his home tongue, but it was the only one he spoke that was used in this tech's realm.

The machine whirred for a moment, "Vrykterian selected. Do you approve?"

"Yes."

It stretched it's legs again, "Good day! I am service model 3892. Would you like to name me now?"

Thrynn lifted a brow and considered, he hadn't thought this thing similar to the creatures of his realm but perhaps he'd misjudged it. He'd seen all manner of sentient beings, after all, some made of wood and stone, others of flesh and blood. Why not one be made of metal? "Do you have a preference?"

"Apologies. I do not understand the question."

Then again, maybe not.

Heaving a sigh, he scanned the shelves. He hadn't expected to have to name the thing. "Keeper."

It did the stretch thing again - it moved a bit like a spider actually. "This is the name you'd prefer?"

"Yes."

"Name: Keeper. Uploaded."

Thrynn watched as it settled again, "Initiate cleaning cycle."

"Scanning." Red beams of light shot from the head area of the robot and stretched to each wall. A few moments passed, "Complete. Select desired outcome." A panel on it's torso pushed out and slid back to reveal a webbing of light that manifested into four selections. Each with varying levels of clean.

Selecting the one that suited him, Thrynn watched as the bot immediately set to work. It was a fascinatingly odd dance. It's four legs picked over refuse while it's hands retrieved anything that constituted a book, scroll or paper. Meanwhile beams of light similar to the red ones that initially scanned the area would burst forth to incinerate debris before it would squat over the pile of dust and ash left behind, lifting it into itself and leaving the floor gleaming in it's wake.

Clever, indeed.

Just as he was about to head back to his living room, the robot approached his scrying mirror and zapped it clean.

Though his muscles ached with exhaustion and his belly grumbled for food, the temptation to check in on his little Human proved too strong for him to ignore.

Ever since she'd fallen dead in the center of his den all those years ago, he'd watched her.

At first it was amusement, he'd seen seasoned warriors lose their minds after falling through a *Caol* yet this little girl, so brave and so bright, had smiled. The fear had been there of course, he would have deemed her stupid otherwise, but she'd fought through it to find acceptance enough to make her way home. Her courage had fascinated him, but it was her soul that drew him in. Her scent, her aura had overwhelmed him with a warmth he'd never experienced before.

And he hadn't been the only one.

He'd sent Rool to guide her home with every assumption the little beastie would be back at his side by morning light, yet the Imp had evidently decided to stick. It had annoyed him initially, he'd thought he would have to intervene and rip the little menace back to his own realm, but rather than fearing the Imp or trying to banish him, little Julia and her family had simply rolled their eyes and opened their hearts and home.

What kind of Humans would do such a thing?

Her blood carried magic within, it was potent and lovely, and because he loved the feel of it brushing at the edge of his senses, her joy in it, he'd helped her. He'd lent her his power, enriching her casting as long as her intentions were harmless or helpful, or pertinent to her growth. And he'd shielded her - a soul as vibrant as hers drew beings of all kinds like moths to the flame.

With a shake of his head, he lifted his hands to activate the mirror. This draw was unlike anything he'd felt in his lifetime, and he found it fascinating even as it embarrassed him. Color swirled and bent as the universe folded back to reveal her, lovely and soft, resting under a thick woven blanket with about a gallon of steaming tea at her side and Rool lounging nearby. As they did most every time he saw her, his fingers rose unbidden to touch - but it was only cool, smooth glass he felt.

His jaw clenched with frustration. Utterly irrational, really. He didn't know why he always hoped to feel the texture of her hair or the warmth of her glowing skin - she just looked so vibrant. So alive. So soft.

The tech behind him buzzed and beeped in the silence.

Ridiculous. Drawing back with a sneer, he forced the aching anger down. He was almost tempted to throw the cursed thing through the window - would have too, had he not had consistent need of it. Rubbing his hand at the twisting pain settled in just above his heart, he turned to leave-

She groaned.

His eyes flashed.

Rool stood from his perch, eyes fixated on Julia, concern radiating from him palpable enough to pierce even Thrynn's frustration. With a whispered word the image enhanced, closing in on Julia close enough to reveal the sweat coating her brow as she winced with pain, her palm pressed to her side.

Nostrils flaring uselessly, Thrynn leaned in close, his hands clenching on the edge of the glass. Something... Lingered. Something had harmed her.

Unacceptable.

His energy pulsed. It was instinctive to send it to her, and he hoped it would warm and soothe her now. Then he closed his eyes, tapping into her magic to feel through her wards, her home, her life.

And it was there.

It was almost... Familiar. Nothing he'd noticed before necessarily, more like something that had been part of the scenery for a long while only now to have been shoved center stage. He could taste it as it brushed and probed her wards seeking a way inside - seeking a way to her.

Intentional.

Focused.

Obsessed.

And right now it reeked of frustration.

"Damn it all..." Thrynn gritted his teeth and shoved the panic twisting his gut aside. Panic! Honest to gods panic, the likes of which he hadn't felt even facing down blade and tooth and claw against the mightiest of the Usurper's Shades-

There'd be time to consider that later.

Right now he needed to focus. Although he could read certain things of it, this interloper was detached. It originated on Earth, it resonated strongly enough that it could only have been cast from a nearby location, but it was almost as though the origin was... Everywhere. Inexact. But it was inarguably masculine-

Thrynn gave in just enough to slam his fist against the wall, sending dust into the air that Keeper immediately vaporized with his lights.

This stranger - it wasn't a natural force. Dark cycles were just as normal as light and just as indifferent. This magic was born of ill-intent. A need to conquer and control. There was no respect there, just raw hunger and rage. The fact that it had shielded it's origin could mean a couple of things: This interloper realized that Julia does not stand alone, that a guardian more powerful than he had gifted her his protection - or his grasp on his own magic was tenuous, his control poor. The remnants were strong, yes, but that could be due to his obvious emotional investment rather than practiced skill.

He would pay with his life.

With one last lingering look at his Julia - for she was *his!* His, damn it, and nothing would threaten her again - Thrynn stormed from the library. He needed to prepare. The shock of it almost gave him pause but nothing could stop this gnawing need rooting deep within him-

He wasn't even sure he wanted to.

It was time he drop this pretense, these games. This watching and waiting- Hell, had he always been waiting?

He'd protected her. He'd taught her. He'd watched her mature and love and live a life full of wonder.

And now he would claim her.

It was time to bring *his* Julia home.

~Chapter Five~

Show Down

September 29, 2021

"It came again last night, didn't it."

Julia sighed and pinched her brow as she waited on her coffee to brew. "Gran-"

"This is weird, Jules. We cleansed you up one side and down the other. No regular attachment should be able to withstand something like that- Dagnabbit Rude, you get out of the way!"

Rude grumbled and stretched like a dog, though he was back to the dragons today. He looked more like Toothless this time than a mini-monster, with slick black scales (thankfully free of that nasty slime) and wide yellow eyes. Actually, he hadn't pulled the slime stunt in over a week and she was pretty sure he was taking on things that he thought would make her happy, which was a sweet concession even if it almost freaked her out all the more.

No one was completely certain what the limits were when it came to Rude. How much did he understand? How much could he sense? The fact that he seemed genuinely concerned and clingy could mean that this taint was far more dangerous a problem than she wanted to admit.

Shoving him away from the laptop so that she could see her Gran clearly again, she chugged some coffee. For the last four weeks these dreams had haunted her damn near every night - and while none had been as violating, as forceful as the first, they'd all been consistently uncomfortable. Frankly, they scared the hell out of her. She felt like she was being hunted, toyed with, like a mouse in the paws of a lazy cat. But before she could even respond, her Gran was already off and running again.

"This darkness? I don't think it's a remnant. It's unlike any memory or spirit I've ever heard of. It's no Imp-" Rude huffed out an offended breath but she continued unperturbed, "Or any other minor Fae that I could name. They wouldn't approach you like this."

"Like what, exactly?" Her throat was still scratchy so she chugged a bit more coffee.

"Like a woman."

Julia winced. While the dreams had ranged from violent to quietly threatening, it's true that all of them held a decidedly sexual element. The being had never managed to get close enough to touch her again, physically at least, though the wounds at her side still ached as she moved and had refused to heal despite her best efforts. She believed their combined efforts to strengthen her wards had helped – Hell, it was probably the only reason this hadn't picked up a notch – but none of them had expected a full on spiritual siege. Maintaining this kind of spell work was taxing, and to top it all off spooky season was only days away. There was just no way she'd be able to make it through unscathed if they didn't shake themselves out of this stalemate.

"I tried to talk to it."

Gran pushed back a riot of gray curlettes in exasperation, "And why, sweet granddaughter of mine, would you do such a fool thing? You know damn well that engaging it may only strengthen whatever tether it has to you."

Julia shrugged.

It had already progressed beyond that, she just hadn't told her family. It wasn't like her to keep secrets, but whatever this was it was well outside their wheelhouse. It had come to her in dreams, yes - and that would have been disturbing enough - but ever since that first night she'd seen it in the waking plane as well. It hovered. Always just at the edge of her senses, close enough to make it's presence clear as it probed the wards she'd set in place. It was flagrant. Unapologetic. Arrogant.

It believed wholeheartedly that she would submit to it's desire and promised rich rewards in return. It seemed to value her in some sick way, and that offered her an element of safety. But she had no clue what it wanted from her or how it wanted to use her – or how far it would go to manage it. All she could do was assume the worst, and the very last thing she was willing to do was offer up her flesh and blood like a shiny new target.

"Well?" Gran waved a hand laden with costume stones big enough to sink a small ship, "Have you learned anything?"

"It doesn't speak. Not with a voice that I hear with my ears. It's more like it casts it's desires into my head. Sometimes the thoughts are clear cohesive messages, but mostly it's just echoes of emotions."

"What emotions?"

Julia sighed and chewed her lip, unsure how much she could safely reveal. Her family loved her, not a one of them would hesitate for even a second before throwing themselves in the line of fire for her sake, and though she hated to risk them even this much she was also well aware they knew far more about working in the dream plane than she did. The truth of the matter was that she couldn't even figure out if the source was Human, or whether this was some angry Otherworlder she'd inadvertently picked up along the way.

"Hunger. Desire. It's always sexual but it doesn't feel like a seduction anymore, more like he's taunting me with it. 'Look what you do to me' - or something like that. He's frustrated. And..."

"And?"

Julia blew out a breath, "I think he's jealous. But that one was weird. The others it was like he willed them to me, wanting me to see or feel it for myself, maybe even guilt me with them, but I'm not sure he wanted to show me the jealousy."

Gran's brow furrowed, "Do you have a suitor?"

Julia barked out a laugh, "A suitor? Cripes, Gran, what century is it again?"

She poked a finger at the screen, "Don't you go poking fun at a woman's age, Lass. I raised you better than that."

Julia rolled her eyes.

"Answer my question."

Julia smirked at her Gran's biting tone, "You're beautiful and you know it."

Her Gran huffed.

"Absolutely stunning, really. I feel blessed to behold you-"

"Now stop that, you fool girl," But she blushed with a cackle, "Don't think I don't know you're avoiding the question."

She sighed, "Nope. My love life is barren and dry."

It was Gran's turn to roll her eyes, "An ex, maybe?"

But Julia was already shaking her head. The few lovers she'd had were friendly connections that burned for a short time and fizzled like fireworks. She'd never felt anything for any one of them - nothing real anyway. She'd enjoyed the fun just as they did and didn't mourn the loss when they were gone.

"You don't know that, Jules. You're always selling yourself short-"

"Gran, this isn't something some random dude could pull off. We're talking about magic strong enough to stand up to the combined power of three hereditary witches - three."

Gran huffed, "Even an ant can get through a door if there's a hole in it."

"Granted, but this is a deliberate probing of our wards. It's a directed message. That's not beginner's luck."

Gran conceded with a haughty nod, "You think it's a witch?"

"Probably. It doesn't feel like a spirit, it's too physical. But for one witch?" Julia shook her head.

"A coven, then?"

"Shoot, Gran. How many covens have you pissed off recently?" She waved off her answering snark, "Seriously, though. I know covens tend to be close knit, but why would they risk the Law of Three in order to help one member get their rocks off? Why the sex? I don't dabble in ill-intent. Never have. There's no way anything that carried my magical footprint could be used to harm."

"Fine." Though she still didn't look convinced, "Have you cast the runes?"

Jules nodded, "It's why I called." Still, she hesitated. "Look, you guys need to listen to me on this one, okay? Don't go rushing into this. You need to promise me you'll lay low, at least until we can figure out exactly what we're up against."

Gran's eyes narrowed on her face, "You've seen something. You don't think it's sexual."

"I mean, it is. Obviously." Julia chewed on her lip, "I don't think that's all of it though. The jealousy - I think it had more to do with my power, our power."

Her brow lifted but before she could do exactly what Julia feared and rush headlong into poking the donkey, she continued, "Seriously, Gran. If I'm right and it's my magic he's after then it follows that he'll shift his attention to you-"

"I'd say, bring it-"

"Or Mom."

That had her quieting.

"Dad's practically defenseless against this kind of thing. You need to ward the farm, get him a talisman and do everything you can think of to protect yourselves. I can't figure all this out if I'm worrying about you."

"Fine. I'll start immediately. But Jules? You will not face this alone. I'll not allow it and neither will your parents."

"I'm telling you, aren't I? I could have kept you in the dark."

"No you couldn't. I know you too well."

Even with all this her Gran could still bring a smile to her face, "Love you, Gran."

"You're the brightest jewel of my heart, Lass." But her face remained stern, "You will strengthen the wards. Light the black candles at night, one in each threshold even those inside. Ginseng and Bergamot for general protection-"

Julia winced, "That tea always tastes like ass-"

"Then add a dash of lemon and quit your complaining."

She rolled her eyes, "Fine."

"Do you have all you need?"

"Yeah, I'm good. You guys?"

Gran nodded, "I'll call this evening. You'll contact me each morning and evening until this is over - and Jules? If anything happens, and I mean *anything* at all, you tell me. You hear? Don't be a hero."

Jules sent her what she hoped was a reassuring smile before signing off. Turning to Rude she sighed, "Well, sounds like we've got some work to do."

Rude perked up and jerked his snout in the direction of the fridge.

With a grateful giggle, Julia rubbed at the crown of his head, "Food first, then work. Gotcha."

After a hearty breakfast, because she needed it even if her hips didn't, Julia settled into her Craft. She'd always loved to practice, the mystique and ritual of it, the sense of security that came with knowing your power and using it. Magic had messed up her life plenty over the years, but it would always be her first true love.

She wove it now, breathing in the fresh scent of the autumn leaves, breathing out her energy until it danced around her in glittering golden waves. Gathering the black candles she placed them at each threshold in her home, before heading into her workspace to piece together four spell pouches. This was the busy work, the mundane, but she wrapped her intent into each one until she could feel each vessel thrum with her energy.

These she took outside, the sun burning bright even through the chill autumn air.

"Hello there, Dear!"

Julia smiled at old Mrs. Ricardo, decked out today in the red and white of her grandson's t-ball team. "Hey! How'd the little man do today?"

"Little slugger, you mean." Mr. Ricardo grinned proudly, "Swept the game, he did."

Mrs. Ricardo beamed, "Oh, he played wonderfully. You should come with us to the next game! Didn't you play little league too?"

Julia chuckled, she'd never once in her life played a sport but there was no point in saying so. "Maybe I'll catch the next one."

"See that you do!" She waddled over, pleasantly plump as the southern peach she sounded like, "What's that you've got there? Something I should worry about?"

Mr. Ricardo eyed the pouches warily then lifted a bushy white brow, "Those for protection?"

Julia smirked and did her best not to show the strain of it, "Just a general precaution."

Mrs. Ricardo patted her cheek, "Can't be too careful, I always say. C'mon Gerald, let's leave the girl to it. I've got brownies to bake!"

"Yes, Dear." Though he shifted from foot to foot uncomfortably, the smile he sent her was genuine. "Good luck with all that, now."

"Thanks, Mr. Ricardo. Tell Jake congrats!"

When they wandered inside Julia turned back to her task, crouching over the soil in the center of the Northern border of the property. Plunging the spade deep into the Earth, she made quick work of it. One pouch for each of the cardinal points, laid in a clockwise pattern. And as she rose from the last, wiping the sweat from her brow, something caught her eye.

In the shadows just beyond the tree line, a beautiful stag stood eyeing her with all the regal aplomb of a king. It's antlers rose to frame his head like a crown, wicked and beautiful in their glory. Feral power was evident in every inch of his frame. He was huge, dwarfing her even as she stood tall before him. This was no ordinary deer, there was no doubt in her mind, but she felt no fear. It was his eyes that caught her. They glittered, the orange and gold shifting with a strange knowing as they met hers.

Her soul shuddered as he bowed, lowering his head before her in regal regard, but she didn't dare draw a breath before he vanished into the trees once more.

Well, that was... Weird.

Unnerved, Julia rushed back to her apartment to finish up. Whatever that creature was, it reeked of the Otherworld - but not in an unpleasant way. It had felt safe, familiar... Warm, even. But what the hell had she done to draw this kind of attention? She frantically flipped through every spell work she could remember doing these past several months but nothing stood out. She'd always been so careful not to engage in any Craft that might bring harm of any kind to anyone. Sure, there were the generic kits of supplies she sold, but those were neutral. They were only tools to be used however the caster wished. Even if someone had followed through with a particularly nasty curse using one of her candles or something, none of that should reflect on her.

She just wasn't that special.

The moment she was safely alone once more she let her freak flag fly, the golden aura glistening back to life around her, comforting her. Finding the center of her home, she stood with arms open and lifted to the skies, heart bared to the wilds as she called to the elements until wind tossed her hair about her shoulders, water poured from every faucet and the tendrils of her plants reached their every petal her way. Closing her eyes, she sent it all deep into wood and stone, seeking the boundaries of her wards and reinforcing any place that felt weak.

Her side throbbed.

For the first time this day - the pain was slight but frustrating. When playing with power of any kind it's best to tread carefully, which required absolute focus. Almost as though it wanted to distract her, every time her magic flared the pain in her side would swell. Like-

Like a calling card to it's master.

The moment the thought hit, something slammed into her wards.

The force of it knocked her clean on her ass, blood trickling from her nose as she gasped for air. In the distance Rude trilled but she was already rolling to her knees, coughing and cursing.

The darkness squeezed.

It was everywhere - *everywhere.* It pressed on her energy at all sides, the force of it wild and frantic. Like a shark scenting blood in the water, he circled her mind, prowling, waiting for an opening.

Julia gritted her teeth and rose to her feet. Stumbling with the effort, she called to the fire and watched as each black candle she'd placed throughout her home flickered to life. Instantly, the pressure reduced.

It was working.

Lighter now, her steps more sure but still weighed down, Julia made her way to the kitchen to fetch the salt.

It knew.

It thrashed and pounded against her walls, each impact resonating through her soul to her skull. She clenched her jaw against it - pain was temporary, and this? It was an illusion. She could break through it - she *would.*

She lined her front door. *One,* she chanted it in her head as the pressure returned like the thing was desperately trying to choke her out. *Two,* the window sill. The fire escape. She coughed, blood dripped from her nose to the floor and she let out a long low moan. Her ribs, it felt like her lungs were about to collapse. Her knees hit the ground but still she pushed. If she couldn't walk then she'd crawl, whatever it took to get this fucker out of her head and home. *Five,* last window. Easier now, each barrier increasing the distance, easing the pressure.

A biting pain appeared behind her eye, forcing a cry from dry lips.

More - just one more!

It shrieked in her mind - the piercing wail nearly knocking her out cold.

Or it would have had Rude not caught her. His energy pulsed around him, an oily green aura that glinted in the chaos. Wrapped in it, her mind cleared just enough for awareness to return. Hauling her over his scaly shoulders, he rushed to the only threshold left unbarred.

"The salt-"

She'd dropped the salt!

But Rude didn't hesitate. Instead his aura erupted into flame, green and glowing, tingling over her skin.

She'd seen this before.

Once.

"Wait, Rude-"

The moment they crossed the threshold between her bedroom and the bath, the world she knew fell away to stars.

The darkness shrieked it's rage into the void.

~Chapter Six~

His

Silence.

He stilled.

It can't be silent - it hadn't been for years - but the void almost screamed with it in his core. Nostrils flare as he delved deep, casting his essence into the Earth to find it once more.

Nothing.

It can't be!

It was the same - just the same - as all those years ago.

He knew *it!*

Rage warred with arousal in a desperate euphoria.

He knew he wasn't the only one.

For years he'd sought her, following the tendrils of her magic as she wove her spells in the night. Insultingly simple, easy tasks. Always so gentle, so welcoming, so kind... So fretful. From the outside looking in, she looked like nothing more than a simple cottage witch – but she rode the liminal edge. She traversed the realms. She held the key to immortality, to power beyond the imagination. Perfection!

He'd known it wasn't just bullshit, no matter what the townsfolk muttered behind their hands. Hell, think of the things they said of him.

They were idiots, every one of them. Ignorant fools grasping at concepts they couldn't understand and wielding what crumbs fell their way like weapons against one another. Mindless beasts, no better than the shit they were born from. Schooling his face into a disinterested smile, he waved at the morons passing by, wandering the streets aimlessly in search of food or work or enlightenment. Pitiful. Humans were pitiful, spiteful creatures so weak of mind and heart they couldn't see the truth when it stood right before their face.

But she was different.

She resonated.

Like he did. Like his true mother and father before that.

She would be his.

The years melted away and he was there again, scenting her for the first time as her frustration heated her blood and brought tears to her eyes. Her soul had lit up like fireworks and he'd known.

He'd begun. He wove spell after spell, anything he could find to capture her attention – to make her see *that they were the same - but nothing stuck long enough to take root. It had been the most frustrating thing. Anytime he targeted her – anytime he drew focus to her – his magic proved impotent.*

It had been the most tangible proof – and the most enticing challenge.

No one had ever been able to smother his magic before. His blood was all but Fae. And while everything he'd learned, he'd learned without guidance, his ability to wield natural magic was as intrinsic to him as the ability to speak or walk or run. And as with any muscle - he'd worked hard to hone his Craft, to discover the truth. For someone to block his will so thoroughly, especially when he was confident they were unaware of his direct intentions... It could mean only one thing: They were more powerful than he.

He couldn't abide it.

Claim it or kill it - but he would never tolerate it.

The beast within wouldn't allow it.

She would be his greatest challenge, his most worthy prize. And when she was his, he would be the most powerful witch in this world once more.

His heart skipped a beat as the thrill of lust pulsed through his core until he shuddered with it.

Oh, yes. This?

This would be so much fun.

~Chapter Seven~

Skittish

Julia landed flat on her face, wind knocked out of her and everything throbbing like a sore tooth. The wildflowers she'd smashed smelled nice enough but they did little to calm her down.

"Rude!"

She couldn't freaking believe it! That little bastard pulled her through the veil. Again!

She gasped, "Prepare-to-fricking-die!" On a groan she rolled to her back and breathed through the pain - she'd probably broken a couple ribs with that fall.

"No more bacon! Ever!" She wheezed it but even that hurt, "You freaking hear me, you jerk? I swear to god I will eat my own boot before I make you breakfast one more-"

A deep resonating chuckle filled the clearing, "Best be apologizing, Friend. It sounds as though you've truly stepped in it this time."

Julia shot to sitting.

It sounds cliche, but the world just tunneled out until colors and scents and sounds blurred into nothing. For a minute - maybe two - there was nothing but *him* and his glinting eyes, and all she could do was gape like a freaking fish.

"Holy crap," The whisper was almost reverent - appropriately so, actually. "What-" Julia choked. *Ow.* Words were difficult around a creature - because he sure as fuck wasn't Human - that was so much... Man.

Holy Cheese Balls...

He towered over her, six-five at least but that wasn't even

counting the horns curling around and up from his brows like the proud antlers of a stag. He was autumn personified - wild auburn locks waved to his shoulders while his eyes gleamed with a feral orange light, the colors rich against the reds and golds of his skin. He wore clothes - thank the gods, she wasn't sure she wouldn't have swallowed her tongue otherwise - but the simple tunic and leather pants did little to hide his powerful build. He was utterly intimidating, but he was also somehow...

Inexplicably familiar.

Arrogant brows arched as he studied her, and she realized she'd begun a sentence. Sort of. She cleared her throat and tried again, "I'm sorry, Sir, but I don't know your name." Mama always taught her to approach a stranger with respect - wild horned Fae especially.

The male squatted low humming deep in his throat until, to her absolute shock, Rude just popped out from the shadows behind her. "No! Wait-" She made a grab for her little dude because she was dead certain that this male, whoever he was, could blink him out of existence without lifting a finger. The sheer magnitude of the power he exuded felt a bit like winding up a tad too close to the sun. It'd burn your freaking face off if he let it. But Rude evaded her and jauntily skipped into his arms for a snuggle.

What... The... Frick?

He grinned as though he'd heard her but she knew she hadn't spoken aloud. "Little Rool here has done well by you, I see. If you would move to protect him so."

"Rool?"

She stared between them, Rool shifting before her eyes to an odd little visage he'd never worn for her before. His skin turned brown, rich and dark as the soil, and along his elbows, legs and about his head a wild red mane appeared almost like fire. He'd shrunk to about the size of a toddler, but his angular face and his glinting yellow eyes clearly were those of an adult - albeit a mischievous one. He looked almost like the Lucky Charms leprechaun - if it nested in *Silent Hill* on the weekends.

When she only continued to stare, unsure whether or not she felt totally betrayed, Rool shrugged a little shoulder and grinned, flashing fang even here among the shadows.

"Aye," The male poked the little Imp in his side and smirked when the little creature cackled his pleasure, "Though Rude, as you've dubbed him, is probably more fitting."

At that Rool stuck out his tongue at the both of us, perched his little clawed feet on the male's forearm and launched himself nimbly into a perfectly executed back flip. The moment he disappeared behind the male's frame she searched for him, but he'd already vanished among the shadows, abandoning her to face his Master alone.

The little prick.

The male regarded her with ageless eyes, unfathomable and strange - and curious. It was unsettling, definitely, but the magics of this world turned their tricks and she found herself calming despite herself. She'd studied the Otherworld enough to know that it was dangerous, incredibly dangerous actually, to let down her guard, but - she'd always listened to that pull in her spirit, that instinct that warned her when she edged too close or too far, and it was quiet now. At rest. At home. She was still freaked out, certainly, but the fear wasn't edging toward panic as it had when the darkness attacked, and she was almost positive that this male didn't intend her any harm - at the moment anyway.

And that energy, it was ridiculous - she knew it was - but god, when it touched her it felt just like pulling on your favorite fluffy old sweater. Comfortable. Safe.

Like a scent you happen across that trips your memory, bringing you back to the atmosphere of a moment in time, the way you felt even if you can't remember the specifics. Your grandmother's perfume, or the way the sun just happens to pierce the windows in just that right way. She'd read that Fae are capable of calming a Human, but it was universally described as a drugged sensation - turning the pleasures of the flesh against you until you are drained, seduced or sedated.

This felt nothing like that.

"Do you know who I am?"

Julia blew out a breath, if she wanted to survive long enough to make it home to Murkwood she was going to have to tread cautiously - very cautiously. Her mother had always taught her to respect the Old Ways, and after her dip through the liminal as a child, she'd all but buried herself in the traditions. She recognized this god - he must be a god with the power he exuded even at rest - but she wasn't quite sure what to do about it. "Cernunnos," She breathed as she lowered her eyes.

What does one do in the presence of a god? Bow?

The male scoffed, "Now that is a name I haven't heard in centuries." Rolling to his ass and lounging back against the soft mound of greenery and wildflowers, he looked every bit the Lord of the Wilds the old texts dubbed him.

"But it is? Your name, I mean?"

When he gestured to another little mound beside him, Julia slowly sank to her knees. She hadn't quite decided whether or not to run, and getting too comfortable in the presence of an old god didn't seem wise for a mere mortal-

"But you aren't, are you?" The male twinkled as he studied her.

"What?"

"A mere mortal. You are much, much more than that."

So he could read minds.... Great! She cleared her throat and deliberately focused on the purple wildflowers to clear her head, "I thought we were talking about you."

He chuckled, "Were we?"

That laugh was almost enough to have Julia meeting his eyes again, she'd be willing to bet her last dime his smile would be devastating, but self-preservation kept her gaze on the ground. "Yes."

"Alright then, Little One. Relax. Ask your questions. I'll answer all that I can."

The command was gentle but the authority was clear. It straightened Julia's spine, "What are you?"

The male tilted his head, "You aren't very good at following directions, are you?" This time her gaze did dart up to meet his, finicky as a fawn, but he enjoyed the brief shine of her golden eyes nonetheless. "Relax, Julia Marie. I mean you no harm. I never have and I don't plan to start anytime soon."

Her delicate brow furrowed, "You know me?"

"Of course I do. Nigh on twenty of your years or more. Do you truly not remember me?"

Shadows, twisting shapes and an openness that shouldn't be there among the corn. The air tasted different, fresher, and it carried a scent - what was that scent? Musk and might and man and spice. There was a voice then, "Calm, Little One," It whispered. And she hoped to God it would help her get back to her daddy.

Julia gasped, "You?"

The male grinned, fang flashing in much the same way that Rude - *Rool's* - had earlier, "Me."

"I-" Gathering her scattered thoughts, she shook her head, "You helped me?" It was nearly unheard of.

Fae hadn't interfered with Humans for centuries, it was a large part of the reason they'd become relegated to folklore. But she remembered the male, though she and her family had always assumed he'd just had a passing fancy for the odd little mortal who'd happened across his path. She remembered the way he'd spoken to her, softly like she was little more than a skittish animal, the way he'd introduced Rude, the way he'd left so abruptly. She'd always figured that Rude had just led her back through the *Caol* she'd fallen through, calling a portal between realms had to be far beyond the ability of any single witch or Imp she'd ever heard of, but now?

Well, here she stood... Again.

Forgetting herself she stared openly.

He nodded.

"But, why?"

She'd been right. When he smiled his whole face lit up with it. Totally devastating.

"Why help a little girl in need?" He lifted a brow, "Why

respond to a shining, fearless soul so bright and open and sweet that I could scarce believe it?" He paused a long moment, watching her, "Why, indeed?"

It sounded suspiciously like a compliment, "Thank you?"

He grinned again, "Are you unsure, Little One?"

She shook her head, "No. No, I'm grateful. I just- That sounded more than a little creepy to be honest."

The laughter was full-bellied this time and just a little shocked. This strange forest seemed to light up with the joy of it, even the wildflowers straightened and danced, and it even tugged a hesitant grin from her.

"Honesty! Now that's refreshing and -" Leaning closer he chucked her chin, "Precisely why I like you."

And he did.

It was a wondrous thing to feel, really - and rare. This simple fondness. Everything about her spoke to her sweetness and her warmth, just as he'd remembered. Her soft brown hair curled down her spine, a little mussed from the journey, though he knew she never truly tamed it. Her clothing did little to catch the eye, little more than a simple black tunic and ill-fitting jeans sporting several holes from wear and tear and dirt staining the knees. No jewels adorned her throat or dripped from her ears to show the world just how worthy she was of such trappings. In fact, she utterly lacked any of the things typically seen among the females of his kind, the tattoos that would indicate rank and specialty, the perfect beauty and grace so expected of a mate. Even his mother had seemed to glide as she walked these halls at his side, shining in the shadows.

But Julia had plopped dead on her ass, golden eyes wide with awe and dirt beneath her fingernails.

He was utterly charmed.

"Hm..." She didn't know what to say to that, but he seemed so at ease it was hard to maintain a good scared. Without conscious thought she found herself relaxing into the sweet grass and wildflowers.

"Over the years my kind have been called many names.

Gods, Fae, Demons and Angels. All of them are as right as they are wrong, I suppose. But you? You may call us Otherkin."

"Otherkin?"

"Aye," He gestured around us, "For this is *Tír na nÓg*. The Otherworld, as your kind prefer. And I am born of it, as you are born of Earth."

"*Tír na nÓg...*" She breathed. She'd known, but it was a different thing to have her suspicions confirmed. Julia stared around at the forest and stone with new eyes, wide fresh eyes. "It's-"

"Not what you expected?" Thrynn chuckled, "Many have said the same as they pass through."

"So… Am I dead?"

"No," The male chuckled just a little, "No, Little One. I would not allow such harm to come to you. You are safe here."

When she only stared, he continued. Although it would be perfectly understandable, he didn't want panic or fear to cloud this first true meeting.

"This land is the wilds between worlds. It's what connects us all, bound to the magic of creation." His head tilted a little, "You may think of it a bit like a tree. This land is like the trunk and Earth just one of it's many leaves. Each leaf represents another realm, some younger, some older than yours, but all are connected through here."

"Is this," Julia swallowed hard, "Is this the only tree?"

Thrynn's smile widened, a proud glint in his eyes, "My people claim that this is but one in a vast forest of trees, so numerous that it may just stretch on forever, growing and changing."

Julia could only stare, it was like talking to God. If there was ever one single Human pursuit throughout all of their sentient history it would be to understand what's beyond this life, and Thrynn just dropped truth-bomb after truth-bomb as casually as someone describing their grocery list. It was simple fact to him, but to her? It was overwhelming.

"But how did I get here?" Julia took in the wilds around her with fresh eyes, "I don't understand."

The male nodded, "It's much to take in. Give yourself time and patience. I will."

That sounded a whole lot like he was expecting her to stay... Which was bad.

Really bad.

She had a home to get back to, a life, people who loved her and a town that was counting on her and her power even if they didn't know it. She couldn't stay here - she couldn't accept that - even if a freaking god demanded it.

If the legends she'd studied were true - which they appeared to be at least hitting somewhere close to target - then time would be a strange thing here. The last thing she needed was to spend a while here thinking she'd only enjoyed a rip-roaring game of mountain bowling Rip Van Winkle style only to return to Earth to find decades had passed while she was away.

"I have to get home."

His eyes flashed even as his brow lifted, "Nay."

She rose to her feet, hiding her trembling hands behind her back, "I can't stay here."

Thrynn studied her, "There is a reason I brought you here. You're in danger."

Her eyes narrowed.

He waved a casual hand in her direction, "Aren't you the least bit curious?"

At just that moment Rool poofed back into existence at his back, rushing over to whisper something in his language - a language this guy evidently understood - to the lounging male. His expression smoothed but his eyes were stony when he turned back to her.

"What did he say?"

Thrynn settled a hand on Rool's head before turning to consider her, "The darkness has retreated from your home. The attack is over but the essence remains. Rool has done what he can to bolster your protections but he still worries for you."

Julia gaped at the little Imp. It wasn't that she didn't know he'd felt some kind of kinship with her, and she'd always known he was independently magical but... This was a bit like hearing your weird-ass family dog had set up a technologically advanced security system around your home. "You can do that?" She whisper screeched.

Rool just shrugged a little horned shoulder and flashed fang.

"I don't even know what to say to that."

"A simple 'thank you' would suffice." Thrynn paused and leaned lower when Rool tugged at his tunic, then he rolled his eyes at whatever the little demon had muttered in his ear, "And he'd like the bacon back - whatever that means."

Julia couldn't help it. This was insanity - complete and utter insanity! Here she stood surrounded by beings of legend and they roll their eyes, mutter and barter for bacon like children. What the hell had her life become? Laughter bubbled, maybe a little hysterical considering the concerned looks she was getting from the guys, but it was unstoppable at this point. Tears welled, and she laughed and laughed until there was nothing left.

"Oh cripes," She rubbed at her eyes and then gave in and just buried her face in her hands, "Oh my god."

A calloused hand, warmer than she'd expected, firmly settled on her shoulder to squeeze with a gentleness that surprised her, "Are you alright, Little One?"

"I need to go home."

Thrynn's brow furrowed, "It isn't safe."

Julia heaved a sigh and finally mustered the courage to lift her face to his, "That's exactly the point."

When he didn't release her she shrugged him off, "I have people who need me, Sir. People I love. If it is as you say and you brought me here for my protection then I'll thank you for it, but that doesn't change the facts."

Thrynn considered her. Over the centuries he'd encountered beings of all different kinds, many of them Human. He'd thought he understood them, but she didn't act like any that had come before. Female or male for that matter. Never once did she ask for his aid, never once did she whine or beg or attempt to hide her emotions in the least. It was... Impressive.

"Alright, Julia Marie. You shall have it your way." When she brightened and began to squirm, he tightened his grip on her shoulder, "Under one condition."

Her face immediately fell and a wariness entered her eyes, "Crap."

"Crap?"

But she only sighed, "I was afraid you'd say something like that."

His lips quirked just a tad. This ridiculous little Human... "Bond with me."

She choked. Hard. He patted her back as she struggled to pull herself together, a bright scarlet flush staining her cheeks. "Excuse me?"

His grin was utterly wicked as he licked his lips, "Not like that. Not yet."

Her heart skipped a beat.

"Agree to a bond. A simple tether. With it, I will be able to feel your spirit, your emotions and your physical being. Should you have need of me, I'll know it."

"I don't-"

"My protection is yours, Julia Marie. I pledge it to you now." When she began to argue, he cupped her cheeks smoothing his thumbs over her lips, "This is the only way that I will agree to send you back to harm's way."

She chewed her lip, "Is it permanent?"

"Aye," Her skin was just as soft and sweet as he'd imagined all these years. How satisfying.

"Why?"

His brow lifted, "Why indeed? My patience grows thin, Little One. I like the look of you in my home. The longer you stay, the less I find myself willing to let you leave."

Rool nodded his encouragement and Julia, though she still looked doubtful, finally blew out a breath, her shoulders bracing for impact. "Fine."

Thrynn's fangs glinted in the sun as he grinned, "Excellent."

His energy pulsed as his palms raised cupped to face the sky. The moment his palms touched in front of him a cornucopia, woven tightly of twigs and leaves, appeared in his hand. Inside was a dark red liquid so thick it looked almost like blood.

Her nose scrunched, "What *is* that?"

He chuckled. He'd laughed more in their short time together than he had this last year alone, he would swear to it. "Wine. Just wine, Sweetheart. Nothing you have to worry about."

Warning bells rang in her head, everything she'd ever read warned in all caps *not* to drink or eat with the Fae. It could drug you or trap you or any number of god-awful things could happen to you, if you did.

As though he heard her, Thrynn dipped until her eyes met his once more. "Those stories also state we cannot lie."

"You can twist the truth. Play games."

He shrugged, "Regardless. I will not manipulate you, Julia Marie. This bond will bring us both nothing but pleasure in the end, this I promise you."

This was a bad idea. A very, very bad idea.

Before she could talk herself out of it, she took the cornucopia and chugged a bit of wine. It was delicious, coursing through her veins hot and tingly like she'd taken a shot of the finest brandy. Sweet fruit burst on her tongue and she hummed her pleasure despite herself. It was... Strangely satisfying to watch as the fae happily downed the rest.

The moment he swallowed that warmth coalesced in her chest, just over her heart, that sweet burn threading itself into a lovely pressure. "What?"

"It's me," He murmured. The cornucopia vanished and his hands filled with her instead, his nose dipping to draw deep greedy breathes of her scent. "You feel me."

"Woah..."

Julia swayed, were it not for his hands at her waist she would have fallen right then and there. But he held her, and it was... Dangerous. The thrill of it shot straight to her core and she clenched, whimpering against the sudden throbbing need.

"I-" She choked a little when his teeth nipped her throat.

Home. *Fricken A, focus Julia!* She thought of her Mom and Dad, her Gran, all of them doing their best to help her. She thought of her home, her business that never did as well as she hoped, her neighbors and Rool.

"I have to go home," But she didn't sound sure, even to herself.

"Just a moment more," Thrynn gritted his teeth overwhelmed by her. He hadn't expected this but -

By the gods, it felt incredible.

Then, before he could take this further than she was ready for, he released her. "Go. Now. Before I change my mind."

Julia, still shell-shocked, blinked wide eyes at him and backed away with a stuttering nod. "Right, yeah. Good. God..."

That wonderful flush colored her skin, and Thrynn wondered at the scent of her arousal drifting in the air. Addictive and lovely.

"One last thing though," She cleared her throat, telling herself that she needed to go even if every instinct shouted otherwise.

Thrynn clenched his fists at his side, his eyes flaring with his magic as he lifted a brow, "Hm?"

"Your name? What should I call you?"

He grinned.

Just like that the tension in the air faded. He reveled in the feel of the brand new bond, sending a soothing calm through to her. Gently, so as not to frighten her when her spine had finally eased some, he reached out to finger her long dark hair.

It was a dangerous thing, giving her his true name. It would grant her a level of control over him that few possessed. He had never considered it with another mortal. He waited for the suspicion to rouse, but, as he'd suspected, none came.

"Thrynn. You may call me Thrynn."

This girl would come to mean a great deal to him, so it would seem.

Basking in her scent, he wondered what it would feel like to take a mate. A queen.

He'd never longed for such things before. After the war, he'd spent years wandering the wilds, exploring the countless worlds it connected and turning his curiosity and energy to the unknown. He'd been voracious in his pursuit of knowledge and a loner. As those of his kind often found a territory to claim, a House to build – maybe it had been grief, but he'd run from it all. He'd always set himself apart from them but... Perhaps he'd been wrong to.

Perhaps this is what they'd meant when they spoke of the Calling.

After all, had he not felt the draw to Earth more times than any other land throughout the centuries? Had he not engaged with Mankind in a more personal, more open fashion than he had with any other race? He'd met countless throughout his travels, those younger and older than Man, those more beautiful and more grotesque. Yet it was always to Man he would return.

Until her.

The moment she'd wandered through the *Caol* and into his den, he'd known. Not rationally. That would come later. But he'd felt the bond take root almost instantly - a recognition of soul to soul - that part of them that is universal, that part which supersedes any physical form. He'd recognized her.

And with it, perhaps, his Calling.

"Nice to meet you, Thrynn."

Her blush appealed to him thoroughly, such sweetness he'd only glimpsed in his long life. He wondered what other lovely surprises she would bring to his world.

"And you, Julia. Finally."

~Chapter Eight~

Escalation

October 20, 2021

On an oath, Julia chucked her pen back to the table and buried her face in her hands. Exhaustion warred with dread as she lingered over her eighth mug of coffee and tried to organize the mass of incoming orders into something manageable. Hell, she would even settle for readable at this point. Funny how people always seem to double down on the spooky business the moment October 1st rolls around as though magic like hers was seasonal and only pulled a Santa once a year.

Rolling the tension from her shoulders, she scanned her workspace. It wasn't that she was complaining exactly - business is business and the wages she earned each fall kept her happy in home for the rest of the trip around the wheel - it just sucked when everything all seemed to come rolling downhill at once. Inventory covered every surface, leaning in haphazard stacks or drying and charging in the sun, binders of invoices lined a bookshelf held together by a couple of rusty nails, a hope and a prayer - but no matter how high the orders piled, or how complex the requests were, she still hadn't managed to shake this damn pressure in her chest.

Whatever Thrynn had done before he slipped her back home, Rude – no, *Rool* - in tow, had left a lasting impression. One that she'd initially hoped would amount to nothing more than the healthy dose of anxiety anyone would expect after a jaunt to the Otherworld. No such luck. It had lingered. Long after she'd plunked onto her feet beside her bed with Rool curled over her shoulders like a ferret and the ghost of Thrynn's teeth at her neck had faded, long after the tension and fear had bled away in the wake of work and the warmth of the morning sun, long after the dreams had come to an abrupt and salty halt – that presence, there just above her heart, had remained. Which meant that she was well and truly stuck.

How stuck?

No idea.

But stuck was never a good place to be. Especially when you've somehow managed to get yourself all glommed onto a freaking god of the Old World. Even a hot one.

And Hell's bells, was he steamy.

Indian food level extreme.

Damn it... Shoving her hair out of her face with both hands she slammed to her feet, annoyed because she had a million things to do and she knew there was no way she was going to manage to tackle a single one of them all hot and bothered like this. She needed to release some tension. Go for a walk maybe? Recharge in the setting sun? She could get behind that and it wasn't like she couldn't use the exercise. She'd been cooped up like a freaking hermit ever since...

Not helping.

Walk it is - though she'd have to make it quick. The last thing she needed was to get caught outside her safe space in full-dark with whatever the heck was watching her prowling just beyond the edge. She'd thought the skeevy stalker was bad enough, but having your every waking moment linked to a creature like Thrynn? That was a whole new ball game. There was only so much a girl could take, really. She was exhausted and jumpy, and she just needed... Time. Numbness. A solid shot of top-shelf brandy. Hell, she'd take all three.

Stubbornly thinking of nothing at all, she slipped on her ratty converse and was just about to shove out the door when the bell rang.

Her brow furrowed. She was almost certain she'd already accepted the delivery she had on schedule for today, and her parents were busy coercing her Gran into going to the doctor for her annual - not that they would bother to knock anyway. Fear kicked in - almost as quick as the sorrow did. Never before in her life had she been afraid to open her door. To friends, neighbors, strangers. This stalker did that. He'd changed it.

And she freaking hated him for it.

"Julia?"

Her brows shot up and she swung the door open instantly, "Mr. Thompson? What are you doing here?"

Travis Thompson sighed, the relief clear on his kindly round face. He'd been handsome forever, in a silver fox kind of way, and she remembered him fondly for the sweet treats he'd always slipped her when he came to her father's poker nights. He was one of those pillar-of-the-community kinda guys, his law office was located right in the town square and his pretty home with it's pretty gardens and it's pretty two car garage sat walking distance from the elementary and the high school. He'd been the one to help Julia set up her business license, and the one to help her Mama out of a hot spot the one and only time she'd had a bit too much to drink and took out a neighbors mailbox with their two-tone station wagon.

He was a good man. A steady, strong, reliable man.

Which made the fact that he looked like a strong breeze would topple him in an instant all the freakier.

White as a ghost and swaying a little, she ushered him inside. Then, because he looked like he needed it and - Hell, she did too - she drew him into a quick hug, gently reading him to check for injuries when his hands touched hers. Healing may have been more her mother's thing, but she could manage the basics especially if something was really *really* wrong. Thankfully though, Travis didn't seem broken or bruised, just rattled. Very rattled.

"Come on inside. Let me get you some tea."

"I-" He huffed out a breath and ran a hand through his thick salt and pepper hair, sending it standing in all directions. "I think I'd like that. Thank you."

She drew him in, settled him at her little kitchen table and sent a silent thanks to the gods that the brews reducing on her stove were floral and smelled nice even if they were a little pungent. Quickly she filled the kettle, put it on the stove to heat and noticed Rool blinking out at her from her bedroom door.

Don't you dare, she mouthed and sent him her best I-will-murder-you-in-your-sleep look.

When he grinned, her eyes narrowed into a glare and she deliberately pulled out Oreo's - a weakness of his - and piled a few on a plate for a bribe. She made certain Travis was distracted, staring out her windows at the sunlight in a daze, leaned down and slid the plate into the shadows under the sink. When Rool appeared she gripped his arm by the elbow tuft, "I swear to God, Rool if you do anything to freak that poor man out I will never get you another Oreo for as long as I live. You hear me?"

Rool rolled his eyes and nodded an instant before he and the plate disappeared.

The kettle whistled, but she took her time bringing Travis his tea and cookies because he looked like he needed to gather his thoughts.

Then she settled opposite him, "Is this about my parents? Did something happen?"

His startled gaze did more to comfort her than anything could have, "What? God, no! I'm sorry- No. Christ." He rubbed at his eyes with the palms of his hands, "Sorry. Language. I'm still a bit... Worked up, I guess."

Julia smirked and laid a friendly hand on his arm, "I've heard worse. What's going on, Travis?"

"Well," He actually wrung his hands together. Julia wasn't sure she'd ever seen anyone do that before. "I guess... Look, I've been friends with your father my whole life. We went to elementary together, high school, college. All of it."

Julia nodded, "I know. He loves you," She said it simply because it was the simple truth.

Travis relaxed some, "I know. I love him too." He took a big gulp of the tea she'd made and then met her eyes, "I know what you are."

She raised her brow and smirked a little, “Okay?”

“I mean, I know that all this,” He gestured vaguely around her place, “Isn’t all just some hogwash to add some oomph to your business model.”

“Okay.” Her smirk grew into a full on grin when he just looked at her exasperated, “It’s not like I’ve been trying to hide it.”

“I know about your mom and your grandmother too. Always have. Ever since Eric started sniffing around your Mama all those years ago.” He shuffled his feet, “I want you to know I’m not here to judge or anything. I never would. I just-”

Julia hummed into her tea, “So you had a run in with the supernatural I take it?”

He blew out a long breath, “Honest to God, I don’t know what I had.”

Rising she refilled their tea and then patted his hand as she took her seat once more. He seemed to need the contact and it bolstered her as well. A sense of dread was starting to swirl low in her gut. She was afraid she knew exactly what this was about.

But gods, she hoped she was wrong.

Because if she was right, then that would mean this thing had reached a whole new level of crazy and she wasn’t sure she was equipped to deal with it - not sure at all.

“We take turns at the office - getting lunch, I mean. Today was my day, and Linda-Gail and Ms. Donna decided they wanted some of that fancy coffee from the Bagels & Brew so I hit there before I made my way across town to pick up our order from The Grill.”

When he paused Julia nodded sagely, “It’s good coffee.”

“It’s highway robbery is what it is,” He gruffed but it seemed to make him feel a little better, “But it’s tasty enough, I suppose.

“Anyway, I’m driving along, right? And everything’s normal. I’ve made that drive, I don’t even know how many times throughout the years, and everything’s normal. It was sunny and that Lana Del Rey, you know the one, she’s got a voice sounds just like my mother and I was thinking how it suited the drive with the changing leaves and the wooden fence posts lining Old Man Gregor's fields.

"I was thinking, 'How pretty'. 'How damn lucky is a man that he can make this drive, listening to such a pretty song on such a pretty day?'

"And then it all..." He rubbed his jaw and tilted his head, gazing blindly at the tea in his cup, "Shifted."

"Shifted?"

He nodded, "Maybe that's not the term for it, but it's the best I've got. It was instantaneous. One moment the sun is there, making everything warm and nice, the next it's like I'd driven dead into the heart of a pounding storm. Rain was pouring down, pushed damn near horizontal by the wind, and that was worked up so good I thought it might've been a tornado. It was thundering too, and lightening. But it was strange. Like it was close enough and loud enough I could feel my teeth rattling in my head when it sounded off.

"The road was different too. You know Cherry-Picker Lane, it's all just blacktop with double yellow lines?"

Julia nodded.

"Well, now it was like gravel. I'd been going a solid fifty - Hell," He flushed a little, "I don't know, maybe it was more like seventy. I just got that little mustang, you know? Martha called it my mid-life crisis but I don't know about all that. I just know it's a fun, zippy little thing."

She smiled to soothe him, "I bet."

He squirmed, "So anyways, the blacktop? It was different. Suddenly it was all gravel or sand - maybe packed dirt, I don't know - but my little mustang couldn't grip it. I was sliding, trying to regain control and something-" He gulped, "Something leaped into the road."

Julia waited, refilling his tea when he chugged it down like it was more than just a few herbs in water. "What did it look like?"

His gaze flicked back to hers, wide blue eyes clinging as he blew out a long breath, "Like a wolf. Huge, though. Damn near the size of my car. And it was wrong somehow, blurry, almost like it was misty instead of furry. And-" He scrubbed his hands down his face with a curse, "It's eyes glowed."

"What color?"

His brow lifted, "What?"

"What color did they glow?" That sick feeling in her stomach had ramped up to full boar now. She knew what was coming but hell if she wanted to hear him say it and confirm the worst.

"Violet."

Julia closed her eyes, "Snoz-balls."

"What?"

"Sorry," She waved him off, "Go on."

He watched her closely and waited a beat, but when she didn't elaborate he kept on. "I slammed on the brakes. I'd barely righted the car when I saw the damn thing, and then I started to slide. There was no way I was going to stop in time - no way. I guess, maybe it was panic - because I was scared out of my damn mind, I'll tell you that - but it was like everything blurred. Everything narrowed down to those purple eyes. But the moment my bumper would have hit it-

"Lana was singing again. The sun was back, the blacktop and leaves were dry and the sky was clear. Blue, save for a couple white puffy clouds."

He shook his head. His hands were still now, as though the telling of it had eased it some, but the rosy still hadn't returned to his cheeks. "I would've thought I'd lost my damn mind. I did. For a minute there, at least. I pulled over to take a breath. To pull myself together. I was doing my best to convince myself I was just too tired or too hungry or too- I don't know, whatever. But when I got out of the car, it was dripping. Soaking wet. And when I went to check the front bumper there were- Hell." He pushed to his feet, "It'd probably be best if I just showed ya."

Julia nodded and followed him down to his spiffy little sports car. Because she knew it would please him she whistled low, "Well if that's a midlife crisis, I'd say you're doing it right."

He grinned, "I'd say. If you're nice, I'll give you a ride to your parents for the game next Monday." He sent her a wink, "And if you promise to bring those little hot wings you do."

"Doesn't Martha have you on a diet?"

He chuckled and rubbed his rounded stomach, "What she don't know can't hurt her."

The laughter died as they rounded the car. Julia's hand whipped to her side the moment she saw it. Memories of tearing pain and brutal strength - all lost to an icy fear.

She did her damnedest to hide it while she hauled Travis back upstairs, while she spelled him a talisman to ward off evil and prepared four spell pouches for him to protect his home, his car, his office, his wife. He watched her the entire time, and to comfort him and bolster herself she allowed him to. Her magic easing from her in shining golden wisps to coil and burrow into the vessels she prepared. When she handed them to him, he eyed them warily for a time before he pulled the talisman around his neck, but when his eyes met hers she knew. Although he didn't understand, not really, he accepted it and he would use it.

That was all she could ask of him.

As he left, she perched on her fire escape to watch. The fear she'd buried came rushing back as Travis climbed into his spiffy little sports car, sending her a wave as he turned towards home...

Three long gouges arcing across the front bumper.

~Chapter Nine~

Unexpected

Cripes...

Scrubbing her hands down her face, Julia tried her damnedest to ease the anxiety clawing at her gut. She hadn't hid it well. She'd tried - she'd done her damnedest not to freak Travis out any further than she'd had to while she prepared the spells and his talisman - but the way he watched her like he'd expected her to explode at the drop of a hat told her she'd done a crappy job of it.

He'd call her father for sure.

He'd wanted an explanation. Hell, he was more than entitled to one considering... But she just didn't have one to give. Any to give, really. She hadn't even been able to promise with any sense of certainty that this wouldn't happen again – for all she knew he could be ripped right into the Otherworld on his drive home this very night. This darkness outclassed anything she'd considered possible at this point – whatever it was even commanded the *Caol* with apparent ease... Something she hadn't thought possible – at least for a Human.

She'd been stupid.

And arrogant.

In all her years of study, the fact that there were powers and beings all across the universe that we didn't understand and could hardly compete with had been made clear time and time again. But her experience with her Craft - it had always been so *right.* So empowering. So fitting. Never once had anything bad actually come of it - Rool included, though she'd considered him a curse more than once. Sure, she'd stumbled a few times, but never so badly that it wasn't something she couldn't rectify herself or with the help of her Mama or her Gran. But this...

For only the second time in her life she felt completely outclassed. And this time, she had a feeling this was no kindly, curious Otherkin.

Lightening doesn't strike twice after all...

Street lights shined like warriors, fighting to keep the darkness at bay as Murkwood bustled and hummed beneath her garden. Cars rolled, people strolled, the scent of food cooking mixed pleasantly with the sounds of kids playing while their parents settled back in for the night. A couple neighbors even sent a friendly wave or a smile in her direction when they noticed her - And gods, she loved it. All of it. She loved it so damn much she wondered if she had the strength to leave it, if it came to that.

No.

Her fingers tightened on the balcony rail until the knuckles shone white in the twilight. Murkwood was hers. This was her home, her people - good people. People that had helped her to grow and love and laugh all her life. She'd worked this land, toiled with spirit and soil, seeded and grown all manner of strange and wondrous things. Her family had history here, a good-standing reputation and a solid niche. They'd more than earned their place - and she would do everything in her power to protect that... Even if that meant doing something really, really stupid.

Opening her eyes she saw him.

She'd known she would.

The stag watched her patiently from the forest, his color shining like the finest gold in the setting sun. Everything about him was majesty, from his towering antlers to his regal bearing. Autumn personified, his power emanated from him to claim this land with all the ease of a king. And then there were those eyes. They flashed like fire with his magic, shining with knowing and with... Comfort?

Yep.

That confirms it.

She's totally in over her head.

Blowing out a breath and steeling herself, she nodded inside - not surprised in the least when the stag poofed from existence right before her eyes. Hell, this night was shaping up to be one of the most bizarre of her existence, and she still had about a billion things to organize and prepare for shipment before the week was out. Still, she lingered... Her eyes drawn like magnets to the West where fire met field and exploded.

And she knew.

It was there. Watching. Seething.

She flipped it the bird and headed in.

Thrynn waited just outside her door, enjoying the thrill that tickled his core at the thought of seeing her again.

His *Anam Cara.*

His soul mate.

It felt almost giddy. With a shake of his head he let out a bemused snort. To think, after all these years of dallying about, countless worlds and countless skirts flipped at his command, here he stood waiting on this little Human with hope and - something wholly shocking - nerves. He wanted her to like him. No tricks, no treats. Just him, for all he was and all he could be.

It was profoundly new.

The thought still left him reeling. His people spoke of the Calling as something irresistible, something instinctive and overwhelming.

A force that shoved you towards your destiny - whatever that may be.

Well, he certainly felt drawn.

If he were honest he had since that first moment, when a tiny Fairy Princess bruised and skittish had plopped into the center of his den seemingly out of nowhere. He'd found her charming then, a beauty certainly, but he would admit that he'd kept her around more for entertainment's sake than for anything else - that's what he'd told himself, at least. He'd questioned it, initially, why he would feel the urge to check in on this little Human or to blend his power with hers to bolster her magic, but as the time moved on and the habit took root, it just became a part of him. An insidious nudge to watch and wait and care. And that... Well, that was wholly unlike him.

He should have known.

The bond tugged at his heart. He could feel her hesitance, but it soothed him to know that all she felt were nerves. Her wariness was completely understandable but he didn't want her scared. Not really. Delving into the bond he could see that she felt the weight of all this too, the pull, she just didn't have the lore to fully understand what was happening to her - to them.

Hell, neither had he.

Requesting the bond had been an impulse. He'd never imagined what that tether would reveal, or the fact that the moment it had rooted within him he'd found himself unable - truly incapable - of keeping a distance. So he'd followed her to her realm, lingered in the forests at the edge of her warding, watched and wondered. Would it fade? This need? This carnal longing? Would he always feel this aggressive urge to protect and defend, to shelter her in his magic and in his arms? Or would it pass given time?

It had only grown.

And with it, his fascination. The taste of her magic, the feel of it brushing his skin, made him yearn for her in a way he'd never thought himself capable. He should hate it, he thought. It should have felt confining or forced. Instead he reveled in the beauty of it. This ache as she teased him from afar, as he tasted her essence in the Craft she wove or the garden she tended - it was maddening. Just as effective as leather and lace.

He was hard all the time for her. This past moon had been torture - watching her smile at everyone, watching her giggle and chat with her neighbors as though that laughter, that twinkle in her eye didn't belong to him. His body longed for hers and it was a violent thing. Everything in him stood at attention, ready to claim, to mate - to brand her so thoroughly his own none would ever look on her again and not see him.

It wasn't unusual for his kind to take mates from all the different worlds they traversed. Their make-up was such that they would adapt to fit their chosen - or vice versa. In this case, Julia would be his. Her heart so open, so breathlessly eager to learn and to grow that he knew she would thrive.

She didn't even know how limited her vision was, how small her world - but no matter. She would travel the realms at his side and celebrate the incredible variety, just as he did. She would have all he could offer and more as they built on the bones of his empire together. She would be his queen, the mother of his children, his lover and his closest friend.

Rapping gently at her door, he smiled as he listened to her stop and suck in a steadying breath.

Yes, Little One, prepare yourself, he thought with a wicked grin.

The fun had only just begun.

~Chapter Ten~

Sharing is Caring

Thrynn knocked.

Honestly, she wasn't sure what shocked her more, that he bothered with the common courtesy or that he respected her door at all. Rool traveled through the shadows, something as simple as a plank of wood and a deadbolt meant nothing to him, but Thrynn was acting like a vampire - *Invite me in, Sweetheart, so I can whisper sweet nothings to you while I drain you dry. Yum yum.*

Julia worried her lower lip between her teeth considering. She wondered what would happen if she just left his butt out there. Would he just... Leave? Break down the door? Poof inside like he obviously could? Would he be pissed? Blowing out a sigh she tip toed to the door, steeling herself to face this obnoxiously gorgeous Otherkin-

As though anyone could prepare for him.

Her breath caught in her throat as she took him in, head to toe. She'd thought he'd had it going on as a stag but *this?* This was on a level all it's own. He'd donned something more Human – the horns were gone, his face looked more normal, softer somehow - but no glamour he could weave would ever totally erase his wild. The clothes he wore looked like something from an Ed Hardy magazine, perfectly tailored jeans and a fitted white t-shirt clung to his frame, doing nothing to hide the fact that he looked for all the world like some kind of massive Gaelic warrior of lore. Even the soft red flannel that he'd thrown over his shoulders only accentuated his arms and hands... Hot damn. There wasn't a girl alive who could handle this guy.

Then he smiled.

She choked-

And slammed the door between them.

His chuckle lilted through the door, "Oh come now, Julia. You know I mean you no harm."

No harm my butt, she thought pressing a damp palm to her racing heart. Heat - it was like her body was on fire, her cheeks and chest scorched raw with it.

Something was happening.

Something totally new.

This wasn't lust. She'd felt lust before and enjoyed it when she did. This was a wanting but it was so much more primal than that. Spiritual. Even as the thought crossed her mind she felt her magic rising within her, unbidden, reaching for him without her conscious will. As though it... Recognized him. Her blood tingled, her hands trembled as power pooled at her palms seeking release.

Seeking him.

"What the-"

"Calm, Julia."

Thrynn gritted his teeth and forced himself to stay still, though it was hard to resist. He could feel her energy calling to him. It resonated deep in his soul urging him to go to her, to ease her desire, to satisfy her - but he held himself back. This was important. He needed her to welcome him of her own accord. It had to be her choice - her initiative. It was vital.

Because the moment she did, he would never let her go.

"It's alright. I'm here."

Even his voice did something to her. Her knees went all weak and wobbly. "Every time you tell me to calm down it only freaks me out more."

He chuckled again though it sounded a little strained, and her magic rose to shine golden before her.

"What the hell is happening to me?"

"Nothing bad. It's only natural-"

"I can't control it."

"Aye, you can." Instinctively she knew the moment he pressed his palms to the wood between them just where her shoulders would be, "You can. Let me in, Little One. I can help you."

Let me in... Those words sent her anxiety spiking, she remembered the way they slicked over her skin like rain on the cliffs that night. Had it been him? Could it have been Thrynn?

No.

She knew it, deeply, intrinsically, as certain as she knew her own name. His essence, his aura was utterly unique. A being could fake a lot of things - appearance, emotion – but there was no shielding the soul. The bond throbbed over her heart and she narrowed her focus to it. It's presence still wigged her out, but right now she delved into the comfort and strength radiating from there. Like a port in a storm, it felt like safety to her.

With a death grip on it, she dredged up her courage, blew out a breath and opened the door.

Thrynn wasted no time. The moment she opened her home to him he caught her, drawing her close as his magic rose to mingle with hers. He barely managed to kick the door shut behind them as the bliss overwhelmed him. Gold and orange pulsed around them like their own personal sun set as he held her to his heart. She trembled against him, and he did as well - his body thrumming with pleasure as her magic stroked and teased.

She gasped, burrowing her face into his chest and drawing his scent deep. "Oh gods..."

"Nay," Thrynn rumbled, "No gods. Only me. Only *ever* me."

He traced her spine to her waist, trailing his lips up the creamy column of her throat as his fingers met flesh for the first time. She erupted, gasping as her magic flared to draw him close - so close to the cusp of something wonderful -

And then she pulled away.

Stumbling back she shoved her hands through her hair and plopped to her ass on the couch, chest heaving.

"Holy crap. Oh, crap. Crap, crap, crap. Okay..."

Julia sucked in air and let it go until she was almost steady again. The pressure was still there, but as she worked to calm herself it felt appeased - not satisfied, far from that - but better... Sorta.

It took him a moment too. *Too fast,* he thought biting his lip hard enough to draw blood. The tiny prick of pain helped to bring his focus anywhere but how sorely aroused he was. If he'd had his way he would take her right here, right now. On the floor, in the hall, against the door - it didn't matter. He'd make her forget her nerves - he'd make her forget her own name, he vowed it.

But he would never take her against her will.

The bond strained with her hesitance and her doubt. She was overwhelmed and frightened, and while the idea of her nervous and waiting for him sounded wickedly delightful, true fear had no place between them. One day soon he would have all of her, but first he would have her trust. There was nothing without trust, after all. He knew. He'd lived alone adrift in suspicion himself for far too long.

And he would settle for nothing less than all from her.

So instead of doing all the wonderful, tasty, delightfully devious things he wanted to, he slowly lowered himself to sit beside her, bringing his hand to her back to calm them both. It felt better, so much better, to have her close enough to touch. "We're alright, Little One."

Blowing out a shaky sigh, she nodded and - maybe despite herself - leaned into him. "Sorry about that," She shook her head, still squeezing her eyes shut hard.

"Oh?" Thrynn lifted a brow and stroked her, "I'm not sorry at all."

She huffed out a laugh, "Used to women attacking you the moment you come to visit?"

He smirked, softening as she finally lifted her eyes to meet his own. "As I recall it was a mutual thing. And something I intend to revisit many, many times once we clear the air a bit."

Julia wasn't sure if that was a threat. It felt a little like one. She also wasn't sure why she felt so totally okay with it. Thrynn had been in her head, her chest, nestled right there beside her heart ever since the bond had taken root, and maybe - now that she'd felt his magic so… thoroughly - maybe even before then.

The fact that he was gorgeous in this regal, princely way could have been easily overlooked had he been nothing more than just a pretty face. She needed substance in her men. Story. Lines drawn in their face from years of laughing and loving and living their lives - maybe a scar or two. And although Thrynn barely had any of that, he most definitely had story to spare. There was nothing soft about him. He sparked so many things within her - curiosity, desire, wonder and comfort - it was like tasting a complex wine... And winding up totally blitzed before you even had a chance to understand it.

His magic felt nice and comfortable right now as it filled her apartment with his energy, but it always rode this edge, like it could tip into terrifying at a moment's notice - and she still wasn't completely convinced he wouldn't turn all that power on her. Fae - or Otherkin, evidently - were known to be tricky creatures. They couldn't lie outright but they wove the truth in deceptive ways until you were so tangled up you couldn't know which way was up anymore. The fact that he was here, this familiarity between them, the way he called to her magic - none of the lore she'd studied had ever mentioned any of this.

"Are you alright?"

His question almost startled her, "Don't you know? Isn't that the point of this," She gestured vaguely between them, "Thing between us?"

He sighed, "The point? You say that as though you believe I constructed it myself."

"Didn't you?"

"Nay," Because it pleased him, he twirled a lock of her softly waving hair around his finger, "All I did was open our eyes to what was already there. We would have discovered it naturally, the longer we spent together. My spell did nothing more than jump start it a little."

Her brow furrowed in a way he found utterly adorable so

he tapped her nose, “Why do you think you came to me - of all places, of all the realms - when you slipped through the *Caol,* hm? Why into my territory? My very den. You broke through every ward I’d laid, every barrier. Nothing should have had that power, especially not a child. Not even a very special child,” He sent her a wink.

“I-” Julia frowned, “I didn’t mean to.”

“I know. I’m not saying you did. That is the nature of the Calling.”

“The Calling?”

Thrynn nodded, “You know it, even if that’s not your term for it. Every living creature does. That quickening in your spirit. That tug just-”

“Here.” Julia pressed a palm to her stomach to ease the butterflies, “Gods.”

“Maybe. Fate is a funny thing.”

He said it so simply. Like he was talking about the freaking weather or a ball game rather than the entirety of her future. Oh man… The panic threatened to rise again so Julia asked the only other question she could think of, “What else does this bond do?”

His eyes softened as he studied her like she was something beautiful, something rare and amazing, like he was still a little surprised to be here himself. “It does exactly as the name implies. It’s a link that tethers us, uniting our souls as one. Through it we can share power, feelings, thoughts-”

“You can read my mind... Even here?” She didn't screech but it was close. She'd known she'd been at his mercy in his realm, the Otherworld crossed all sorts of barriers, but here? Truthfully she hadn't thought of it until now, but she'd assumed that he would be tethered at least somewhat by the bounds of this place.

He only grinned, “Only when you wish to share them with me or when you're particularly emotional.” When she still looked thoroughly uncomfortable he leaned forward, cupping her cheek to draw her eyes to his, “It goes both ways, Sweetheart.

You and me, we're in this together."

"Bull."

"Bull?" He scoffed.

"I can't feel you. I haven't heard anything from you." Even as she said it, she knew it wasn't true. Wasn't that what she had followed to pull herself back from the panic just minutes ago? Touching a finger to her heart she realized she could see it - sort of. Not with her physical eyes, it was more like an awareness in her spirit. It was undeniably there, a braided thread shot through with the colors of their essence as it tied the two of them together.

"I have," Sheepishly he lifted a hand to the back of his neck as he cleared his throat, "I have been blocking it. I didn't wish to overwhelm you."

"Well, A-freaking-plus on that one. Cripes…" She pulled away, jumping to her feet to pace. "Okay, if you can do that I can too, right? Show me."

His face darkened, it was almost like the light got sucked from the room, "Absolutely not."

"Excuse me?"

"I will not have you hiding from me. Especially not now when darkness lurks at your door." When she looked as though she were about to argue he rose as well, gripping her chin gently and forcing her to meet his glowing eyes, "I will not risk you."

Julia gulped, she wasn't ready to let it go, not by a long shot, but he was right. They had more pressing things to deal with at the moment. "Okay."

He searched her eyes for a long moment before nodding decisively, "Tell me what happened."

She did. She told him everything while he lounged on her couch, waving a hand to light candles when night fully fell around them.

"He was scared, Thrynn. To the bone. I've known the man my whole life and I've never seen him scared like that.

"It's escalating. I don't know why it picked Mr. Thompson but the way he talked about it… I don't know. It could have been a mistake."

"There's every possibility that the man just happened to be in the wrong place at the wrong time." Thrynn steepled his fingers and tapped them to his lips, "Portals are tricky things. They aren't tied to any specific element so no creature, that I know of at least, is born with the innate knowledge to use them. My people, we train with portals when we near our Proving – the day we show our clan that we have achieved all that is required to be considered an adult. Most of us take years to master the *Caol*, even with guidance."

Julia bit her lip, though she dreaded the answer she forced herself to ask, "Do you think this is an Otherkin?"

Thrynn considered, his brows furrowing as he stared into the flickering candlelight. "I'm not certain... This is an individual, male or at least very masculine in nature. I've been monitoring his activity since the night I realized you'd been harmed and his energy has always originated here – on Earth. That certainly doesn't mean he couldn't have come here prior to all this but it's unlikely, and if he's being used as a conduit of some kind there would be a tether to the Otherworld."

Julia slapped her thigh before rising to stomp to the kitchen, "None of this makes sense! Why us? Why me? I've never done jack-all to invite this kind of attention-"

"Calm, Sweetheart. We'll figure this out."

She ignored him, "I believe I'm still the primary target but-"

"You want to be." Confusion colored his words as he watched her busy her hands preparing the kettle for tea, "This darkness is dangerous and strong, yet you want to be the focus of it." He tilted his head, "Why?"

She didn't answer, instead she just prepared her tea poking at the tea strainer to make it steep faster.

"Wouldn't it be safer, clearer, if it's focus were the town?"

Julia shook her head, "Murkwood isn't perfect but there are good people here. Honest people. People who respect the land and the cycles and their neighbors. They don't deserve to take the brunt of this chaos when they don't even know what it is."

"And you do?"

"Better than they do anyway. Besides I-" Julia broke off, a little shocked herself at what balanced so precariously at the tip of her tongue.

Thrynn leaned forward, gripping the couch in his fists to keep from crowding her. He could sense it. A breakthrough. A small crumbling in the wall she seemed so determined to keep between them. "Besides?"

Julia dropped her gaze to her tea, "I have something they don't."

"Your magic? While your power is impressive and growing, you are not equipped to stand against this. You must know that."

But she was already shaking her head, "No. Not my magic."

"Your family?"

"Well yes, but anyone who knows even the most basic facts about me would be aware of them. Anyone with any ability to read energy or feel magic would know about us. They love me, and they'll stand with me but they aren't warriors. We aren't warriors."

Thrynn waited.

"Rool has always been around, I believe he'd help if he could – or if he felt like it. He's not exactly the most reliable." Julia chewed on her lower lip for a moment as she considered. It was risky. This could be construed as a request and the last thing she needed was to wind up in debt to a minor god. But Travis' story rang in her head, her people hung in the balance and they... They were worth it.

Straightening her spine, she lifted her head to meet his gaze head on, "I have you."

Thrynn sucked in a breath, a brilliant smile curving his lips. It was a tiny victory, but he'd never felt more a man than at just that moment.

Her eyes met his for a long moment as she waited for him

to say it. To count the cost. To ruin it. But he only watched her, softly, his energy sparkling and safe. It felt a little like giving in when she chugged her tea and strode over to him, but it also felt good and she needed that right now. Especially for this next part.

She flopped back beside him, worrying her lip between her teeth. He gently tugged it free with his thumb, unable to keep from touching her despite the way she stiffened. "There's more. Something you aren't telling me. What is it?"

Julia hesitated, the dreams were embarrassing enough as it was without Thrynn's level of intensity boring down on her. She didn't know how he'd react – would he flip out? Pity her? ... Deem her tainted somehow?

She felt tainted.

The wounds at her side throbbed just to spite her. A painful reminder that she'd been branded, however unwilling. Like a dog pissing on it's territory.

The shame of it all weighed on her. She should have been able to protect herself, she should have been quicker to reject the things this shadow had made her feel, she never should have come at his command. It didn't matter that she hadn't wanted it. She'd submitted.

And now a tiny voice she didn't know she had wondered if Thrynn would throw her away.

The thought stung more than she cared to admit. "Okay, but you have to promise not to freak out."

He growled, his face darkening, "Not a good way to start, Little One."

"Fair enough, but I'm serious." Delving into humor for comfort, she curled her knees to her chest and poked him. "I can't afford to replace my stuff so you have to promise to keep it cool or take it outside."

His eyes narrowed but he didn't move, "I saw you near this Thompson's car. What did he show you?"

Julia sighed, "Alright." When did her mouth get so dry? "This all started around mid-September. With dreams." When his brow furrowed her fists clenched-

Just get it out there. Get it done. If he leaves and you're alone, you're no further back than when you started.

And that would make *him* the asshole, she reminded herself. Better to know it now than to figure it out later, when whatever this was between them was too far gone.

"They were... Sexual. Seductive. He forced himself on me – Like he was showing me that I had no choice, that it would get better if I just gave in."

"How many?" Thrynn gritted it out, his claws lengthening in time with his fangs. It dared? It dared touch her against her will? The dream plane was as real as any realm, should one know how to traverse it. His mate... Unacceptable.

Her brow furrowed, "What?"

"How many times did he contact you?" How long had he missed it? How often had his mate been harmed because he'd been off gallivanting across the realms?

Why had he denied this truth for so fucking long?

"Seventeen. But the first... That was the worst." She watched him closely but he only worked a muscle in his jaw, "It started nice, tempting even. But it was wrong. I felt this need to trust him, to give in to all of it, but it was wrong. I didn't even know his face." She winced at the memories, the violation, the pain. Her side throbbed, "When I broke away from it's grip in the dream there was pain. Along my back and around to my side. Like a punishment."

Steeling herself she lifted her shirt just enough to show him the remnants of the marks, "You promised not to freak out," She said quickly as his eyes flashed. She tried to pull her shirt back down but he wouldn't let her, he wouldn't even look away. To distract him, she hurried on. "Travis' car had the same cuts. Almost like a calling card."

His nostrils flared, his breath harsh as he fought to contain the beast within. His every instinct demanded he stand, fight and destroy anything that dared bring harm to what was his but his enemy wasn't here now.

Julia watched him with wide, wary eyes.

Right now, his mate didn't need a warrior. The time would come for that - and it would come soon, he promised himself - but it wouldn't be this night. Tonight she needed his softness, his shelter. She needed to know that he would see to it she would be safe in all ways. Always.

Reaching out he laid a gentle hand over the angry marks, his magic flaring beneath his palm to dance with the candlelight. She sucked in a breath when he touched her. "The only mark you will ever bear," He murmured leaning close to rub his nose against hers, before reaching around to nip at her ear with his teeth, "Will be mine."

~Chapter Eleven~

Betrayed

Something's changed.

He'd known she would be upset. It had been an accident, bringing that man into his world. He'd needed a run, needed an outlet so that she didn't see how maddening her efforts had been.

She'd managed to block him – it wouldn't last. Not forever. Already he worked to erode the barrier that kept him from her mind.

Sweet. Smart. Seductive.

He'd brush against the energy of her wards sometimes, just for the thrill of it, but then she'd gone and tainted it with something. Feminine, delicate, but unwelcome.

It was only Julia he wanted.

He'd needed to get away. He'd needed to go somewhere he could express his frustration freely so that he could regain control. She needed his control. She'd want it. Expect it. And he wanted to give it to her.

He wondered... Did his slip up with Travis make her jealous? Did she feel this maddening too? Did it frustrate her?

Is that why?

It felt like an invasion.

He would know her magic anywhere. It had been rich before - like dark chocolate, milky and heady and sweet. He'd immersed himself in her essence for decades. Watching and waiting while it matured... The perfect pair to his own. Every so often that feminine taint would color it but it never lasted – never insulted. But something's changed. Something lower. Underlying. There was something new there. It felt almost... Feral.

Betrayal.

No. It couldn't be. She wouldn't do that to him - not after so many years, not when he'd shown her time and again how much he had to offer. He'd waited and watched, preparing himself as a witch and a man to bring her to heel.

She would submit to none but him.

He vowed it.

Whatever this was - it was a sickness. An infection invading her spirit and riding it's coat tails to glory.

Understanding dawned, he nearly swooned with it. Of course!

This was to be his first challenge!

He would free her of this parasite and then she would see.

She would finally *see* him.

~Chapter Twelve~

First Meal

Julia's side tingled beneath Thrynn's palm, his magic dancing gently across her torn skin. Her eyes widened as she stared into his, and then a sudden flash of pain had her back arching away.

"Hold." He came to his knees before her, gripping her hip with his other hand to keep her still, "I know. I'm sorry." Thrynn tipped his forehead to hers, "Only a moment - just a moment, Sweetheart."

Julia gasped, tears welled. Spilled. It felt like he'd jabbed needles deep into the antagonized flesh, like he'd torn the broken skin anew. But she could also feel it working.

This was different, definitely different than what talents her mother had – more honed, more thorough. No mirror wound stained his shirt with blood, the pain didn't spark in his eyes, it didn't consume her tip to toe the way it did when her family had broken the bond. Gods, but what kind of power did Thrynn truly have? It was terrifying.

Orange flashed – the piercing ache peaked.

And then it was gone.

The pain receded as quickly as it had come, then the tingle, then the heat. Finally, breath heaving and fingers trembling they stared into one another's eyes in the quiet. Close. Entwined. That had been more than a healing, more than a simple spell to help or to bind. That had been strangely... Intimate.

Julia cleared her throat.

Thrynn jumped back so fast it was almost comical. He leaped from the couch and, if it hadn't been utterly ridiculous, she could have sworn she saw his face go beet red.

He cleared his throat and made a bee-line for her kitchen before she could see what she did to him - or before he could do exactly as she feared and wreck the place. Everything in him wanted to own her, tame her, hold her down and force her to take all he had to give panting and pleading beneath him – but that would make him no better than the asshole that had marked her. Energy pounded through his veins hot and fierce, priming him for a battle, for a claiming that wouldn't come - not tonight, at least.

Not until she was ready.

To calm himself and for the sake of his sanity, he directed the excess energy down sending it deep into the wood of her floorboards, walls and ceiling to encase them in a small nest of his own. When his magic brushed up against the wards she'd already set in place, it felt perfectly right. A welcoming softness that blanketed the frenzy until it too fell dormant within him.

Too fast dammit, he scolded himself as he forced himself to still, until his heartbeat returned to normal. That healing – it had been no different than any he would have administered to a wounded ally and he'd assumed it would feel just as distanced. Foolish. Everything between them was still so raw, the last thing he wanted to do was frighten her more. Bracing his palms on either side of her fridge, he sighed. Never once in his memory had his control been tested to such a degree, and she wasn't even trying.

"Are you alright?" Julia sounded tentative. She wasn't sure what had happened but when she touched her side, the skin now perfectly whole for the first time in months, she'd felt something incredible shift within her. For those few moments he'd opened himself to her, and his violent need had left her breathless.

It still freaked her out, most definitely. Only a fool would taste something so wild and feel nothing but flattered.

But mostly, it had turned her on.

Biting her lip, she hesitated only a moment before touching his back softly, "Thrynn?"

It was like every ounce of tension left him at the touch of her hand. He softened and plucked something from her fridge before turning to face her once more, his confident smile firmly back in place. "How about pizza?"

She blinked, "What?"

"Pizza? You know, round bready thing all dripping with sauce and cheese?" He waved the Domino's magnet in front of her face, "I hear it's delicious."

"You know about pizza?" Julia fell back to lean against the counter, her arms coming up to cross over her chest. Talk about left field, "What are you talking about?"

Thrynn stepped toward her, chucking her chin with a little grin. "Feeding you, Sweetheart. And myself as well." He didn't mention that it was the only sure-fire way he knew of to procure sustenance in this realm in this century, or that he'd only figured it out when he'd gotten hungry enough to halt a delivery boy and steal his package for himself.

"You want me to buy you pizza?"

To his credit, his nose only curled for a moment. That she would imply such an expectation on his part would be a grave insult among his people, a proclamation that she found him lacking in his ability to hunt or provide, but she was not his kind and couldn't know about any of that. "Of course not. Go. Rest. I'll take care of everything."

Her brow furrowed, "But- Do you even have a phone? Money?"

He only sent her a haughty sniff and waved her away.

"Okay then," She stared him down for another long moment but when he prodded the bond she didn't seem afraid.

Actually she seemed more at ease than she'd been before, just very confused. Perfectly understandable, considering. Since that evening weeks ago when he'd first seen the pain in her eyes he'd watched, but never once had he seen her suffering. She'd hidden it well. Masking it for the sake of friends and family, perhaps even for herself - but it had to be a relief to be free of such a scar.

"If you're good for a couple, I'm gonna go shower."

An image of water and steam coursing over her pretty olive skin shot straight to his cock. Because he wasn't sure he could speak without making a fool of himself, he nodded. She hesitated another beat, "Thrynn?"

"Hm?"

"Thanks." She waited until his eyes met hers and kind of nodded toward the couch, "For healing me, I mean. And..." She fought the urge to bite her lip again, "For everything else too."

Then, before he could haul her close once more, before he could even respond, she sent him an awkward wave and backed into the bedroom, closing the door behind her.

Thrynn blew out a long breath and shook his head before reaching for her phone, this little female was sure to be the death of him. After struggling for a short time with the little contraption - he'd seen similar things in his travels but had never needed to use them before now - he placed the order and settled in to survey her set-up.

It shouldn't have surprised him, considering how fascinating he found it's mistress, but he found the modest little dwelling wonderfully inviting and unique. He paced every wall, tracing a finger along the little trinkets and knick-knacks that colored her apartment, her world, her life. Photographs peppered each wall, painting them with adventure and love and laughter. Her garden spilled from every window, the herbs and flowers adding a fresh, rich spice to the air, and he could feel her energy twining through the leaves, candles and crystals as they charged in the moonlight. The space was comfortably cluttered but clean - both spiritually and physically, he noted with a small smile. She'd built a fine den.

He looked forward to what color she would bring to his own.

The longing sang in his heart but that was for another day. Thrynn was well aware that his presence was making her tense, but allowing her time to rebuild those blasted walls she seemed so intent on was unacceptable now. Not anymore. She would learn soon enough that there would be no going back - not with him.

Still, he didn't think she would put up much of a fight. He listened to her splash about in her shower, cleansing herself and calming her nerves. She was no ordinary Human, after all. The gift rode her blood as it did his own, and she'd grown adept at listening to the push and pull of her spirit. And she was painfully honest. In fact, he couldn't think of another being he'd met in all his years so utterly lacking in guile. She'd felt the draw to him, and although he could see it embarrassed her she'd done nothing to hide how he effected her.

That was trust.

The perfect beginning. Already she looked on him with hope and familiarity, she recognized the feel of his power bolstering hers in her Craft. Soon enough their bond would grow until they would be so entwined, body and soul, that none would ever be able to stand between them again.

Had he not harmed her so, Thrynn could almost thank this interloper. It may well have taken him several more years to bring her to him had he not threatened his claim. This had been the swift kick in the ass he'd needed to pull from his own routine, to begin to make a change. A change he'd craved. A change he'd longed for ever since his clan had fallen, leaving Yvelta empty save for the corpses and the memories.

The delivery boy arrived, the promise of sustenance and sharing readily drew him from the sorrow that always tainted thoughts of his family, of Yvelta. Perhaps one day, when things were built anew and fresh life and love echoed those halls, the sadness would leave and only the positive, only the lessons would remain. It was a hope he harbored close to his heart, one that pulsed through the bond despite himself.

That was what she was to him: Hope.

He answered the door, sliding a single gold coin across the young lad's palm and weaving a minor illusion to make him leave.

"I saw that."

When he turned back she leaned against her door frame, arms crossed enticingly over her chest and a pretty smirk curving her lips. She wore simple coverings, soft and tight enough to cling to every curve of her long legs. The shirt was clean, if a little tattered, and sported a symbol that resembled a crest of arms – yellow, green, reds and blues. She'd made no effort to entice him, but his mouth watered all the same.

Mischief glittered in her eyes so he grinned back before hauling his prize to the table, "No harm, no foul - I believe is the term."

"That's going to come straight out of that kid's pocket."

Thrynn shrugged, "The gold piece is more than enough to pay for such a meal in any realm, I assure you."

"I bet," She sniffed and then gave an appreciative sigh, "Pepperoni. Thank the gods."

"Nope, just me."

She rolled her eyes and went to fetch plates and throw on some tea, "Please. And that gold will only do him any good if he can figure out how to trade with it."

Thrynn blinked, utterly baffled. "Since when do Humans not know how to trade with gold? Heavens, I haven't been gone *that* long."

Julia just rose her brows and snorted.

The shower had worked wonders on her nerves and she'd come to a few major conclusions in her mind. Well, maybe it was more a state of tenuous acceptance, but still.

The way she figured it, Thrynn and her obviously had something going on that sourced well beyond either of their understanding. She'd seen the shock in his eyes, felt his wonder at his own responses to her through the bond. He'd loved it, embraced it - and as far as she could tell he was genuine, which meant they were in this boat together.

And she was honestly just *really* happy to not have to face this darkness alone.

So, she figured, one thing at a time.

Pouring their tea and bringing everything over to set up a

couple spots at the table so they could eat like civilized Human beings, she plopped into her seat and gestured for him to follow suit. He hesitated behind the chair, his eyes flaring as he seemed to consider for a moment. Then he nodded and sat with a flourish and a smile so easy going, she couldn't be sure she hadn't imagined that weird hesitation before.

"So, I guess we should probably talk about this guy-"

"Nay," He shook his head and loaded a plate with food, laying it in front of her before filling a plate of his own, "Not right now." He would not have this interloper tainting this meal.

Their first meal.

"O-kay..." Julia knew damn well something had happened, his intensity had shifted, focused – she just wasn't sure what had peaked it. She could only hope that sharing food in this realm didn't mean the same thing as it would in the Otherworld, at least according to the myths she'd read. Otherwise, dude was even stucker than he'd been already.

But Thrynn only grinned at her.

She wasn't wrong, not completely. It wasn't that he was trapped here, but enthralled? As surely as had she mixed a potion of her own. He just didn't mind in the slightest.

Thrynn rode the thrill of it as he settled in to share a meal with his mate. Humans had labeled the food and ritual mystical in and of itself, but there was nothing particularly binding about the mechanics of it specifically. Meals were simply a sacred thing to his people. They're bonding, the core of the hearth and home. To share in the spoils of the hunt is to welcome him as family, to have set such a pretty place for him in her home so casually - it was a step.

A very important step.

Slowly but surely she was coming to accept his protection, his power, and his presence in her life. It was an encouraging thing, and it ignited an instinct within him that had always been there, riding him even as he rode the currents of time and space. Alone.

He'd always been alone.

Of course there were others of his kind that wandered, but they were few and far between. Rogues. Drifters. His kind were naturally territorial, it was inherent to their role as guardians of the wild realm. They did as his father before him, claiming a land, a people, a family for himself and defending it fiercely until his dying breath. In his grief he'd thought it a foolish thing. The more that lean on you, the more leashes tugged at your collar - but this feeling she inspired in him... It wasn't foreign. It was deeply rooted, calling to the core of everything he was and ever had been. Perhaps it wasn't the presence of leashes at all that bothered him, as he'd once believed - perhaps they simply hadn't been the right one.

He needed to be needed by *her*.

Thrynn watched Julia as she chomped an overlarge bite of pizza, smiling with her eyes as she chewed. When she murmured an apology and a slight flush crept over her cheeks as she dabbed her lips with a napkin, everything within him lightened. In that moment, he swore to her and anyone else that might care that there would be nothing - not in this world or any other - that would bring harm to her or those she loved.

They belonged to him.

With a chuckle, he reached over to thumb a little tomato sauce from the side of her lip, heat sparkling in his eyes as he licked it away himself. When her own magic flared in response - reaching to caress him despite her best intentions from the look of it - something else caught his attention as well.

His scent had changed. At first it was so subtle he hadn't fully been aware of it, but now that he sat immersed in her, basking in the ebb and flow of her energy as it toyed with his, it's true purpose became clear. His body readied itself for her, and urged hers to do the same. It lingered, potent and tempting on the air, exotic and enticing. And she felt it. Her eyes glinted in the firelight, her breathing slowed and evened as a lovely flush pinked her chest and cheeks like rose petals. A moment more and her scent bloomed, rising to tease alongside his own.

But her eyes were wide when they met his, "What is this?

What's happening to me?"

His nostrils flared. He could feel it it riding just beneath the longing and the lust. Fear. So he just sighed and brushed his fingers down the back of her hand. Only for comfort, nothing more. "Nothing is wrong, Sweetheart."

Her brow furrowed, she dropped her hands to the table and shoved back, leaning as far as she could from him without actually leaving her seat. "This isn't normal."

He tilted his head, "What do you mean?"

"I mean," She gestured vaguely at the table, the home, him, everything, "You! You being here? Wanting this? This is *not* normal. Even for me and I've made weird my thing."

To ease them both he gave her the space she seemed to need, relaxing back to take a happy bite of his own food. "Just because something is different for you does not mean it's abnormal," He said it simply, like a professor correcting a student.

Julia scowled, "I'm not talking about cultural philosophy here." She slapped a hand to her chest, "This? It's like I can't control my responses to you. My magic just goes off without any effort on my part, my heart is racing. Hell-" She slapped both hands to her thighs and wiped. Hard. "Even my freaking palms are sweating! That's not a normal thing. I mean, sure you're hot. Smoking, really. Any woman with half a sex-drive would be all over that, but-"

He grinned wickedly and chucked her chin, "'Hot' is it? It pleases me that you think so."

"That is *not* what I meant."

His brows lifted and, because it pleased him, he trailed his fingers lightly over her cheek to tuck a stray strand of hair away. "It's what I mean. You are the most beautiful female I have ever seen." Leaning close once more he trailed his nose over her throat to savor her sweet scent – just a moment more and then he would let her be. "The most fascinating. The most captivating-"

She shoved at his shoulders. "Bullshit," But she was laughing as she said it.

He grinned. This playfulness called to him and he was not above taking advantage of it while he could, "Not at all." Moving fast he leaned over her, bracing his hands on either side of her chair, trapping her easily. "I'd show you, if only you'd allow it." With a fang that glinted like a weapon in the candlelight he nipped at her chin, "I'd take you to places you've only ever imagined." He groaned a little when her desire perfumed the air, his fists clenching on the arm rests to keep from touching her, pushing her, "Further than."

Julia sucked in a breath at the promise - and it was a promise she believed wholeheartedly he could deliver, cliché as it may sound. His scent overwhelmed her, crisp and masculine and so effing hot. The butterflies in her stomach roused into a full on frenzy and heat zinged straight to her core leaving her wet and wanting. Gods, but she'd never felt so *much* before. Ever. It was like her body had been on stand-by, just existing until he swooped in to unlock it.

"Oh man," Her hands whipped up to his shoulders - to pull him closer or push him away, she wasn't sure - but her fingers curled into his soft tunic when he smiled... That freaking smile-

"Eff it."

Reaching up she slammed her lips to his - maybe someday she'd look back and wish she could have been more suave, or tender or elegant, but at the moment she didn't care in the slightest. His surprised chuckle vibrated through her an instant before he took control, sweeping her under with a barrage of tooth and tongue.

It sounded ridiculous, even to her, but he was literally intoxicating. Her mind spun until everything around them, everything but him faded into nothing but background noise - and that was softness.

The moment his tenderness gave way to desperation, she was lost. Utterly consumed and totally fine with it. His taste was wickedly addictive, a sweet-heat that lit fires with every dominating stroke of his tongue. It burned a little too, in a lasting way - the way a good brandy does when it hits your throat and warms you from the inside out.

The Earth was moving – or they were. Hell, she couldn't tell anymore and didn't care.

He lifted her from her seat so smoothly her legs had wrapped his waist and her had circled his neck before she'd fully realized it. They'd been reduced - they were nothing more than instinct, motion, pleasure. On a shuddering sigh, she buried her fingers in his thick auburn locks and pulled until he gasped at the sting of it.

"Yes, my Julia." Thrynn bared his fangs, the pain only fueling the frenzy she inspired. She was madness personified, fucking glorious with it, and he was well-ready to lose himself in worshiping every soft curve and dip of her.

But when he began to carry her back to her room, she pulled away, "Wait! Wait. Crap."

She shoved at his shoulders, "I know, I know. Sorry. Gods, I can't think when you touch me." His grip tightened on her ass, locking there hard enough she wasn't certain he would do as she asked. Damn it, she didn't mean to tease. She'd never meant to crawl up him like a tall, dark and handsome tree either, but the moment had gotten away from her. It wasn't that she feared the sex – fuck, she craved it – and if he'd been just another guy she would have tackled him to the ground herself.

But this was more than passion. Something else was here, something more.

A heaving breath passed, then another, before he buried his face in her throat and lowered her. Slowly. Ensuring that every inch of motion was contact and fire as her feet dropped to the floor. When it was done, he loosed a low growl that she felt vibrate straight down to her bones.

Although it hurt her - *actually* hurt her - she backed away from his hands. Shocked and more than a little impressed that he let her go.

Thrynn stood, chest heaving, eyes squeezed shut as he forced himself to quiet.

"Maybe you should go," Julia all but choked on the words.

She didn't want him to - in fact that may be the very last thing in the world she wanted him to do - but what tiny fragment of her sanity remained demanded she at least throw it out there.

"No chance in Hell," He gritted. Her relieved sigh did more to steady him than anything else could have, "I'll not leave you again, Julia. Not now."

Not ever.

"Okay," She chewed on her lip and gestured to the basket of blankets beside the couch. "There's stuff there - Um... Hold on." With both hands up as if to ward him off she backed into her chamber, "Just wait there."

He smirked and forced himself to relax, the calm returning as his heartbeat finally slowed. So it wouldn't be now, that's fine. Anticipation was half the fun, after all. She wasn't ready, he thought as she shoved a pillow into his arms that smelled of her and fidgeted with the hem of her shirt.

"I'm just gonna," She gestured over her shoulder and cleared her throat when he only continued to watch her. "Thanks for the food."

"My pleasure, Little One," He rumbled, amused when she nodded quickly and slammed the door shut between them as though that flimsy barrier could do anything to hold him at bay. "My pleasure indeed," He murmured as he turned to the couch, the throbbing heat still clawing at his core. Perhaps this was just what it felt like to find your *Aman Cara,* he thought.

She's not ready. But she would be.

Very, very soon.

~Chapter Thirteen~

Where We Come From

October 21, 2021

A loud bang and a vicious curse woke Thrynn early the next morning. Brilliant sunlight filled the living room, warming his skin as it lingered on his bare chest. The night had been a rough one, the couch about a foot too short for a male his size and images of Julia haunting him well into the wee-hours. Blearily, he blinked open heavy eyes to find Rool perched on his haunches, his face hovering two inches from his own. "For the..." He groaned and shoved the Imp hard enough to have him tumbling to his little ass, "Can a man not have a moment's peace?"

He heard Julia snort and sat up quickly, his heart skipping a beat at the sight. By the gods, but she was a vision. All the reds and browns of the forest shone in the tumbled waves of her hair as it fell wild to her waist, and sleep still softened her eyes. She was lovely, her limbs long and lithe like a feline, though she stumbled in her fatigue as she made her way to the kitchen.

The fluffy spread he'd found last night bunched at his hips, a welcome barrier when Rool righted himself and hopped up to lounge beside him. The visage he wore today was a strange one, some cross between a bird and a lion. Like a Griffin if it were ugly and small. His wings were tucked at his sides, his body a splotchy black and gray because it seemed he couldn't decide between feathers and fur. His little head was almost his natural face, pointed and toothy, bare but for the little halo of mane that was a weird greenish color today instead of his usual red. He also smelled...

"What in hell is that?" Thrynn muttered, absolutely disgusted when a foul ichor seeped from Rool's skin and onto the couch below.

"Dammit, Rude! How many freaking times do I have to tell you-"

Rool straightened, mischief gleaming in his eyes as he swung his long thin tail in her direction, flicking the poof at the tip.

"Don't you pull that crap with me." Julia warned and muttered something incoherent about not even having coffee beneath her breath. Even she wasn't fully sure what she'd said. Slamming into the cupboard beneath the sink she dropped the cleaning spray onto the table with a thump and slapped her fists to her hips, glaring at the little creature. "Proud of yourself?"

Thrynn almost smirked when Rool twirled in a circle, flicking his tail in her direction as if to say *absolutely*.

Julia pursed her lips, "That's fine. Cool. I guess someone's not having breakfast anytime soon."

Rool froze in the middle of his parade.

"No bacon, no eggs," Julia waited, her grin spreading evilly when he met her eyes. Then she shoved the real dagger home, "No waffles."

Rool's eyes went wide and, to Thrynn's absolute shock, he leaped over to grab the cleaning spray before begrudgingly cleaning up his mess with a mutter all his own.

When he was done, Julia still didn't appear wholly appeased, so the little Imp disappeared into her bedroom before tromping back out to present her with a little shiny trinket of some kind.

Which would have been enough in and of itself, but something else had Thrynn jumping to his feet in rage. "Why the hell did he just come out of your bedroom?"

Julia's brows rose as she surveyed the six and a half feet of half-clothed furious male glowering at her from her living room. His hair was all rumpled and sexy, and with those jeans unbuttoned and hanging from his hips like the could slide to the floor any second? Oh, man. Because she needed it after a night of dreaming about… things, she chugged half a cup of scalding coffee. "What?"

"Why," Thrynn's voice was little more than a growl, "Did that Imp walk into your chambers so casually?"

Julia's brow lowered in obvious confusion and she looked at Rool who just flashed fang and lapped at his paw like a house cat. "I mean-" She cut off when Thrynn stormed over to grip Rool by the scruff of the neck, "Whoa! Whoa, man. Can we all just calm the hell down, please? It's like-" She blinked at the digital read out on the stove, "Cripes… It's only six in the morning."

She couldn't remember the last time she'd seen six am, but she was damn sure she'd pulled an all-nighter to do it.

Scrubbing furiously at her eyes, she turned to start hauling stuff out of the fridge for breakfast. If she was going to have to deal with drama, she had no intention of doing it on an empty stomach. Thankfully it appeared that Thrynn had turned his ire on the little Imp. They spat words at one another - she'd freaking *known* it was a language, the little bastard - while she heated the stove, stirred the batter and switched on the waffle-maker.

When a girl has a hulking pissed off Otherkin camped out in her living room, an Imp in the closet, a stalker hell bent on taking her down and about three hundred orders to fulfill in the next three days she figured waffles were only appropriate.

"What the hell do you mean that's where your nest is?" Thrynn bellowed and Rool actually jumped, skittering to hide behind the couch. Then he turned on her, "He's got a *bed* in your *chambers?"*

Julia downed the rest of her coffee, "Well…" She sent a baffled look in the Imp's direction but he was thoroughly hidden. "I mean, yeah…"

"You allow him in your private chambers?" Thrynn was flabbergasted! And more than a little furious - not at Julia but at Rool. To infringe on someone's privacy in such a way was a horrendous over step. His mate, his *Anam Cara*, had been spied on for years by the little bastard and-

Apparently he was the jealous sort. Who knew?

"Has he watched you change? Watched you sleep? Watched you touch yourself?" He threw it out there so off the cuff, she choked on her coffee.

For her part, Julia was starting to feel really, really uncomfortable. His questions flustered the hell out of her, the blush burning like fire as she thought about the sleepless night she'd spent all hot and bothered by the hulking Fae snoring on her couch.

Had Rool ever watched her?

Over the years she'd become so used to his presence it was almost like he'd become... A pet? Maybe? A dog or a cat. She'd definitely changed in front of him, though he'd never acted particularly affected. But, she almost choked again, had she touched herself while he'd been in the closet? She'd always been careful not to bring lovers around him, but that was more for their sake than out of any sense of modesty. Honestly, she wasn't sure what the little dude had seen over the years, but the way he was going pale and backing away from Thrynn right now didn't seem all that innocent.

To distract herself, she plated the breakfast and hauled everything over to set the table while the Otherkin glared at one another in her itty-bitty living room. Her very small, fragile living room. "Guys?" When they ignored her she cleared her throat, "Guys!"

Both of them paused mid-sentence to turn to her.

She gestured to the table, "Breakfast is ready."

Rool poofed in happiness, skittering into the shadows behind the couch and reappearing a moment later as his normal, leather skinned, fire haired self to plop down in his seat at the table.

Thrynn though gaped at the pretty little kitchen table, utterly stunned. "You prepared all this? For me?"

"Well, I expect you to share..." When he didn't respond Julia scanned the food, trying to figure out whether or not he was offended. "You have a thing against waffles? I mean, I'm no chef but I know how to make waffles."

But he just stared. This was so much more than the pizza had been the night before, simple though it may seem. She'd taken the time, put forth the effort to craft this for them with her own two hands - it was intimate, sweet. Whether she realized it or not, her work showed him affection and acceptance. The kind that he had not felt since he was young.

"I-" Shaking his head, he claimed his seat. Even the Imp's presence did little to shake the tremor in his chest, "I have not enjoyed a meal such as this since my mother passed. I-" He cleared his throat and, because he needed it, reached over to brush his fingers lightly down the back of her hand, "Thank you."

"Sure." Julia chewed on her lower lip and went to refill her coffee. This was clearly another one of those things, like last night. Something important was happening here but she couldn't be sure exactly what to make of it. Still whatever it was, it seemed to have gotten Thrynn's mind off of Rool's nesting habits so that's something. Not one to look a gift horse in the mouth, Julia came back around to join them at the table, "Were you close? With your parents, I mean."

Thrynn's whole demeanor just... softened. "Aye."

When he didn't elaborate she poked her fork in his direction, "Can you tell me about them? I didn't even know that Faefolk had families - not the way we do, at least. Do you have siblings? Pets?" Somehow it was hard to imagine Thrynn as a little kid, sleeping in a room filled with toys and posters and a fat, snoring dog while his mom made breakfast before school.

The way Thrynn lit up, it was sweet. Really sweet. Julia had always wanted a family - when you come from something as full and rich as she did, it was hard not to - but at twenty-seven years old she'd spent several years watching the kids she grew up with marry and start popping out babies, and... Well, with Rool and her work it just hadn't seemed to be in the cards for her. She'd thought she'd come to terms with it. She *had* come to terms with it.

But watching Thrynn and feeling what she did for him… A little ray of hope took root.

Insanity.

Almost as if he knew, his eyes flashed as he grinned, "Aye. My people live long lives so children are rare, but my parents were blessed with five of us. I am the youngest."

She smiled, "Are you close?"

The light in his eyes dimmed just a little, "No. Not after…" He cleared his throat and sipped at his coffee.

Uh-oh.

Even Rool hung his head as though he sympathized with his master. "Sorry," Julia stuttered, "I didn't mean to pry."

"Not at all," Thrynn offered her a gentle smile and touched the back of her hand, "The memories are good ones. It's just unfortunate, what came in the end."

"Oh." She waited.

"There was a war. Many centuries ago in the way this world keeps time. Several Houses rallied together to march on my father's territory. The land he ruled held many gateways - Earth's included. He had access to resources and technology that many of our people simply didn't. It made us a strong, wealthy clan. The envy of his peers." Thrynn paused and considered his coffee for a time, "But envy is a dangerous thing.

"My father had been in good standing with our High King. They were friends and he supported the crown openly. So when war came, he and my House stood to defend his reign. I remember the army as it collected on that final day. It was horribly impressive, my father donning the traditional armor of our House, as did my mother and my brothers while I was to stay in the care of my sister as I was yet too young to battle. To look on them - it felt as though nothing could shake their claim. But the King fell that day.

"Mythraal ascended. He demanded that each House loyal to the former King be stripped of their titles, their lands. My parents died defending their home, as did three of my brothers. My sister fled, she would have been forfeit to Mythraal's harem should she have stayed, and I helped her. It's what saved my life."

For comfort, and because the bond throbbed with a kind of grief Julia could only thank the gods she'd never known herself, she slipped from her seat and into his lap. It wasn't sexual, just... Human. Wrapping her arms around him, she drew his face to her throat, cradling him there and running her fingers through his hair. When he sighed and nuzzled in she whispered, "I'm so sorry."

It sounded ridiculously empty.

"It's alright, Sweetheart. It's been a long time now." Still Thrynn basked in her comfort. Right here? It was the most whole he'd felt in years.

"But you're still here. How?"

"I returned. I guard my father's most favored territories unbeknownst to the Usurper. I've never attempted to officially claim a territory, and I've spent many years wandering among the worlds. But even so, I've always done what I could to protect what's left of my home. It's what they would have wanted."

"How?'

He smirked, "Subterfuge mostly. My father had a reputation for prosperity, but he was a skilled soldier and an intensely private individual. The truth of how and where he'd amassed his holdings has always been a secret, one that I guard to this day. If the Usurper knew of a place so rich as this-" He gestured to the world outside, "He would surely do everything in his power to claim it for his own.

"Mythraal is not a kindly male, his ego is vast and very fragile. Humans have come a long way since last I walked this plane, it's true, but your people still couldn't hope to stand against even a small selection of his Shades, let alone any of our true military. So I've done what I can to hide the truth of you and others like you from him."

Julia squeezed him closer, utterly rocked. It was a terrifying thing to think that mankind's place in the greater universe was so vulnerable, that all it would take was the wrong being stumbling across their lands for everything to fall into chaos.

She had no doubt he was right when he told her no Human army could hope to stand against a royal House of the Otherworld - Hell, some people couldn't even wrap their heads around other life in their own universe as of yet.

"Thank you," She murmured. It seemed the only fair response. If it were true, she and all her world owed him dearly. "I have no idea how to repay you for something like that."

Thrynn only pressed closer, his arms wrapping around her waist as he curled around her. "No need, my Julia. Only being here, with you, is prize enough for me."

~Chapter Fourteen~

A Message

Julia lingered on his lap for a little while longer, but when emotions calmed and the heat rekindled, Thrynn placed her back in her seat, unwilling to let her hard work go to waste. As she settled back into the rhythm of the meal, his openness and his generosity grew all the more clear. He shared everything with her, having her sip from his coffee or nip at his fruit. When she'd asked him to pass the butter, he'd just buttered her waffles himself without so much as missing a beat. And all the while he chatted, poking at Rool in the language they spoke and gently coaxing smiles from her. He touched her constantly, pressing his knee to hers or brushing his fingers over the back of her hand or cheek. It was easy and fun - she wasn't sure how he'd managed it but he'd smoothly dominated her morning, shoving all lingering thoughts of the encroaching darkness from her mind.

Thrynn babbled something at Rool then scoffed and rolled his eyes to her when the little Imp shrugged an indignant shoulder and chomped into a piece of bacon. "So Little One, Rool here tells me he enjoys your family. Your father especially."

Julia snorted, Rool had a special hard-on for freaking out her father. Eric Murphy was what people around here called good stock. A very solid, stoic type. It was probably what made him so perfect for marrying into a line of witches, come to think of it - and he'd always held rock steady. There wasn't much that could shake the man. Time and again Rool had thrown everything he could think of his way, and my dad had just heaved a sigh and waltzed right on through it like it was nothing more than a weird kid playing weird-kid games.

Pretty on point with that one, actually.

She had so many memories of her father wielding bat and broom - and even once a vacuum - to try to shoo Rool away from her closet at night. And every time it hadn't worked he'd just scratched his head, grumbled a bit and made him up a little plate of breakfast in the morning.

"Hasn't managed to shake him yet." Julia winked at Rool who rolled his eyes, "Never going to either."

Thrynn studied her, "Both of you speak of your kin with such affection. Tell me, what of the ó Súilleabháin line? What's it like to be a Murphy?"

Julia's brows rose, "Seems like you pretty much know all there is to know about me already."

He waved her off, "Nay. I've watched and I've listened, but to say that I *know* anything at all would be remiss. It's," He cast about for the right term, "Distant. Removed." He nodded to the television, "Like watching a story play out on your picture box. I want to know the heart of it."

"Why?"

He grinned and leaned in, tucking a strand of hair behind her ear, "Why?"

"This thing between us. I don't even know what to call it but-"

"A bond," He supplied helpfully.

"Okay, sure. A bond," Though that didn't feel totally accurate.

When Julia shoved a flustered hand through her hair, Thrynn gestured to Rool to make himself scarce. This was for them and them alone. She hovered on the brink of acceptance, waffling back and forth between following her instincts and trying desperately to force them to fit into Human terms.

"But what *is* it? You feel it too, I can tell. You were just as surprised as I was when you showed up yesterday and-"

"I wouldn't call it surprised. Pleased? Aroused? Intrigued? But not surprised."

Her face went flat, "You were surprised."

He chuckled, “Alright. I hadn’t realized the Calling would feel quite so... Demanding, I suppose.”

“Demanding.”

“Mm-hm...” Because it pleased him he claimed her hand, toying with her long, clever fingers.

“What do you want from me? What do you mean 'the Calling'?”

Heat lit in his eyes. Fangs flashed as he leaned in close, stealing her breath as he cupped her face, tilting it up until his lips ghosted across hers to tease-

The windows imploded at her back.

Glass and rain shot into the room like gun fire, tearing through everything they touched. Thrynn tackled Julia, taking her to the ground and shielding her body with his own. Wind roared and something screamed - it wasn’t her. Her breath was gone, ripped from her by the shock.

The darkness - it was *here*.

She felt it watching her. Not with eyes, not in a physical sense. It was more an invasion of soul, of intent. Her stomach gripped and twisted as though it had taken hold of the very core of her and pulled, wanting her closer, wanting to own her.

“Fuck off,” She gritted out, shoving Thrynn from her body as she rolled to her knees. Forcing her head down she called her magic, relishing in the wild rush of it as it throbbed through her veins to surround her in shimmering champagne gold. She took the instant of quiet and gripped it by the balls.

This was her *home.*

This was *her* town.

And this darkness?

It had no idea who it was messing with.

With a guttural sound of rage she’d never made before, she shoved to her feet. Her power pulsed out to encompass her home until the winds and the rains were forced outside once more. The quiet clouds of the Autumn morning had been tainted, black and violet swirled and writhed almost as though creatures shoved at the thin smoky barrier with frantic tooth and claw. She would get rid of it - this jerkface had no place here, no *right.*

But when she started toward the fire escape, Thrynn shoved her behind him. “Shades,” He scanned the storm. Impossible… It couldn't be! She shoved at his arm, fighting to get past. “Nay. Don’t exit. It’s what he wants.”

Every inch the warrior, Thrynn looked braced and ready to draw a freaking sword and rush into battle, even as blood from a thousand tiny cuts seeped from his skin. His intensity is what stalled her, he wasn’t telling her no - not to control her - he was assessing the threat.

“He?”

A muscle worked in his jaw as he approached her barrier, scanning the street. His magic rose with a hiss when he found exactly what he was looking for, “Aye.”

Hc gripped her wrist when she joined him and sucked in a startled breath at the sight. “A Grim,” She breathed horrified.

“A message.”

The thing was only a shadow, shaped to send a message to his female, heavy-handed and melodramatic after such a violent display of power. It stood apart from it's writhing, screeching brethren rushing within the storm. A huge hound, it’s fur black and shifting like the furious clouds it formed from, stared at them with violet glowing eyes. Intelligent eyes. It sat dead center of the crossroad, perched arrogantly on it’s haunches as though it knew it’s success was inevitable - it’s intent clear.

This way lies death, turn back.

Thrynn wondered for a moment whether or not this witch knew that Humans once used crossroads to contact him personally in the old days. He’d done nothing to mask his presence here, in fact when he’d layered his magic over her own wards the night before he’d deliberately let his essence shine through. It was a claiming - and this?

This was a challenge.

He glared at the storm, “The source isn’t here.”

As though it heard him speak the Grim lifted it’s head,

shining violet eyes snapping as it loosed a feral growl and bared it's teeth.

"Oh no."

Julia gripped his arm, very nearly shoving past him and onto the balcony beyond, "Mrs. Ricardo!" She hissed out a curse and shoved at Thrynn, "No! Mrs. Ricardo! Wait!"

An elder, a woman draped in soft cotton, hunched against the rain as she made her way to the parking lot. She made no move to respond, just tucked her head and shuffled quickly past the windows, past the pretty little gardens-

Finally, Julia ripped free of Thrynn's grasp, throwing herself to the fire escape to shout for the woman- "Mrs.-"

Julia...

The moment she broke the barrier of her home, the interloper gripped her. Air hardened around her, invisible but as immovable as stone. It held her fast, the rain like spikes slamming into her skin. Dimly she could hear Thrynn shouting for her as he beat his fists against whatever hold this thing held over her. She felt nothing.

You can save her, Julia.

The voice was the same. The deep, resonating growl from her dream. A shudder skittered up her spine as she recalled the painful pleasure, the tearing fire of it's touch.

You can save them all.

Gods, it didn't hurt but it should have. She felt her feet lifting from the ground even as tears spilled from her eyes. It twisted her, her face forced away from Mrs. Ricardo and to the silent, lurking madness of the Grim. It tilted it's head.

Come to me, Julia. Give yourself to me...

Forcing her eyes shut she focused, her magic narrowing to the darkness that wrapped her. Starting small but hard, like acid eating through flesh, the gold spread.

The hold wavered.

She wobbled in the air, a marionette flailing on the end of a faulty string – but she kept going.

Cease! Stop this. No!

It screeched when she dropped, retreating with an angry whine an instant before Thrynn finally broke through the barrier, wrapping his arms around her and encompassing her in a shield of his own magic.

The Grim erupted.

Roaring loudly - it's maw gaping wide to reveal wicked, dripping teeth and a darkness so absolute it looked almost alive - it came to stand. As Julia shuddered in his arms, safe and sheltered from the punishing rain, Thrynn called to *his* element.

Fire, mighty and cleansing, engulfed the puppet. Pointless, it was nothing but a distraction, but Thrynn knew how to send a message too. The pain would pierce it, would echo through to it's master-

And yet it never moved.

It's eyes held theirs, fury mounting.

She felt it reach for her – she felt it's call as it pressed against the shelter of Thrynn's energy – so she added her own to bolster their shield.

Silence.

There should have been a roar, a growl – *something*. But it was only silence as the Grim ripped it's eyes from Thrynn to meet her own.

Then it lifted it's paw, slowly, almost as though it were disappointed, before slamming it back into the ground. Violet lightening shot from the storm, slamming into Mrs. Ricardo.

Julia screamed.

The woman's body lifted and jerked. Her limbs dancing horribly in a mockery of death.

Cookies scattered, the pretty little red and white tray bearing the emblem of her grandson's little league team fell to the side, soggy and forgotten.

Julia screamed as the Grim turned it's back, as the wind retreated, as the rain calmed. She screamed as the clouds rolled away, as the morning sun reached out to warm her icy skin.

She screamed.

And then she cried, curling into Thrynn as he swept them

both inside.

~Chapter Fifteen~

Unleashed

Rool muttered something low, his skin morphing from the leathery bark of his natural state into the soft, silky fur of a cat. He only took on this visage when Julia was seriously upset, it was his offer of comfort and compassion. Thrynn watched the little Imp nudge at his mate's arm until she finally uncurled from the tight ball she'd wrapped herself into, perched on the corner of the couch.

Her sobs cut at his heart, worse now that they'd quieted to this hollow, tired ache. Her helpless fury and fear saturated the bond and, for the first time in a very long time, he had no idea what to do. Part of him wanted to rage, to destroy. It urged him to hunt down this threat and force him to endure every ounce of agony he'd inflicted on his mate - three-fold. But another part - the stronger, deeper part, the part that already twined his soul to hers - it called for his comfort. He couldn't leave her, not even if she'd begged it of him. His very heart demanded he stay, nurture and protect.

Red and blue flashed outside her apartment, casting the walls, the photographs, plants and tools he'd found so charming the night before in a harsh unnatural light. At least the sirens had ceased - small miracle that. He'd held her, enduring every quiver that throbbed in time with that shrill chorus of tragedy. Life swarmed around the death outside, curiosity and sorrow mingling to taint the air.

Julia shuddered, finally uncurling just enough to allow Rool to crawl into her lap where he purred like he'd seen normal cats do in the movies. He was warm this time - a little too warm to be normal, but the effort was there and she could appreciate that. She stroked his fur and chewed her lip, selfishly drawing what comfort she could from Thrynn's magic as it cradled her, gently pressing to her skin even as he stood sentinel at her surviving windows like some dark guardian angel.

She didn't deserve it.

None of it.

His effort, his affection. Even Rool's gentle attempts to soothe her made her feel like a heel.

You can save her, Julia.

Mrs. Ricardo was dead. Her husband had only just quieted, but his wailing would echo in her mind for the rest of her life. She'd been loved. Important. She'd been a mother and a wife, a lovely little woman who always made too much food and shared it with the tenants of the building just because. She'd been a grandmother, the last time Julia had stopped to chat with her she'd practically glowed with pride because her eldest grandson had just played his first little league ball game -

And now she was dead.

It was her fault.

If she'd reacted faster, said or done something more - Hell, if she'd done *anything* at all - Mrs. Ricardo would still be here, straightening her husband's tie and cheering on her grandkids at the park.

Tears welled, drenching Rool who blinked up at her with concern in his weird little eyes.

"Why?" She choked on it, her throat shredded.

Thrynn turned to her, moving so fast he all but blurred as he suddenly knelt at her feet, big warm hands cupping both her knees. "My Julia..." He murmured.

"Why did you stop me?"

Confusion lowered his brow but he'd seen this before. Warriors, survivors torn with guilt. Patiently he wiped the tears from her cheeks, cupping her face in his hands, "Julia."

You can save her, Julia. You can save them all.

That fucking voice echoed in her mind - jarring her.

"I could have-"

But Thrynn shook his head, "Nay, Little One."

"It wasn't her he wanted! It was me-"

Thrynn moved his hand around to firmly cup the back of her neck, "Nay." He waited while she sputtered and shoved at him, waited until she'd quieted, submitting to his hold. "Nay." There would be no questioning it. Not now, not ever. "That's not true. You know that's not true."

"He was-" She shuddered, she would have dropped her head if Thrynn had allowed it, instead she just closed her eyes. "It was punishment."

"It was *his* choice." He squeezed her neck until she met his gaze once more, "His and only his. Make no mistake, he will see judgment for what he's done."

When she did nothing but shake her head, Thrynn squeezed. "Tell me you understand." In this there could be no compromise.

"I-"

Gritting his teeth he tilted her head to rest against his, "It was wrong. It was awful and unfair. But it was not your fault. Say it."

"It was not my fault," She mumbled it to appease him but, shockingly enough, the words actually helped. Maybe it was the bond, maybe he was doing something to make it work, but it was like a ray of sun breaking through those black fucking clouds - an arrow of truth.

"It wasn't my fault." Stronger this time.

Thrynn was *right*.

This guilt, that's what the bastard wants her to feel. He wants to use it to force her hand, to frighten her, to shake her control because-

She'd won.

She'd denied him.

She'd fought him and *won*.

When he'd gripped her, she'd broken his hold. When he'd ravaged her mind, she'd refused.

The bastard dared to force himself into *her* territory and threaten *her* home? He thought he could just waltz in here and make demands, and nothing and no one could stand in his way?

Bitch please, she could call to the elements too. She had her family at her back, Thrynn at her side - Hell, she even had Rool. Lifting her hands to Thrynn's wrists she gripped him, her eyes steady and hard and glowing into his.

And now?

Now she was pissed.

If it was a fight this fucker was looking for, it was a fight he would get.

"We'll make him pay."

She couldn't wait to watch him burn.

~Chapter Sixteen~

None but Him

Fuck!

A male?

Another fucking male?

How could she?

All these years waiting and working. Watching and wanting. How many sleepless nights had he spent, cock in hand, hard and hungry for her?

He'd been so fucking *patient - so* fucking *kind.*

She'd just needed to mature - to reach zenith - so that she could be claimed. Her power was so pure, so familiar that it resonated in his blood like water. Refreshing, bolstering, strong.

But…

She'd fucking RUINED it.

It was muddy now, tainted and foreign and-

Him.

He practically growled, barely cognizant enough to direct his raging energy into the pavement beneath his boots so that no one could see. He felt his fangs lengthening as he gritted his teeth -

"You alright there, Man?"

Idiot.

Fool.

Fucking moron.

Just another swine led to slaughter by road signs and TV ads. Humans - the thought nearly had him sneering at the guy - they fuck up everything they touch. They don't understand respect. Hell, they couldn't even begin to grasp-

His heart stalled.

Shoving his sunglasses further up his nose, he grinned as his eyes flared with his power.

That's it!

"Fine," And he meant it.

That had to be it. His Julia had been raised among Humans, her father even was one. This confusion, this slip - it was the only explanation. The only thing that made sense.

She'd always been weak. It had been one of her more charming traits, the softness so mixed in with her natural power. He'd always intended to maintain it - to use it. He would be her spine - her compass – and she would be his sword. All that power, she only needed him *to direct it.*

To master it.

Evidently this fucking male had decided to do the same.

But he didn't know *her. Not like him.*

He hadn't studied and prepared - walking these streets, enduring every slight, every presumption. He hadn't immersed himself in her-

He never would.

It would be easy. He'd scented the male's energy, he could find him now. Study him.

Remove him.

She needed direction - it wasn't her fault. Not really. The Humans had misled her - it was no wonder her tender heart led her astray.

She would learn - Oh, he would enjoy teaching her.

There would be none for her but him.

~Chapter Seventeen~

Unfair

Thrynn watched Julia warily as she picked through the debris. Her tears had ceased, thank the gods, but a quiet seething had taken their place and he wasn't sure that didn't disturbed him more. This anger, it was unnatural for her. Julia was no born warrior. The blood lust within him had always been there, waiting, preparing him to protect and defend, to kill - but she carried none of that. She was softness and light, her heart a precious refuge, warm and safe.

Now she was warm - undoubtedly - but there was nothing safe about this heat.

He sensed a change - something very, very dangerous - and it didn't shame him in the least to admit that it frightened him.

"May I help?"

She startled. Though he'd spoken softly his voice had cut through the tension like butter, tossing the room into an unsettling resonance. "There's not much we can do, really. I'm going to have to call my landlord, but there's no way anyone will be able to come out this late- Gods, how am I going to explain this?"

A warm hand stilled her and when her eyes jerked up to meet his, Thrynn had crouched before her. "There's no need for that."

Her brow furrowed.

"Move back, Sweetheart."

When she complied he breathed deep, letting his soul vibrate in tune with the soil down below. It was different here - it was different everywhere he visited - but the elements remained the same. The vibration in his heart grew as it met and melded with the song of this plane until it rang loud enough to fill the space with a low thrumming sound.

Then he let his energy flow.

Thrynn's eyes closed. He focused on the memory, directing his will to paint her home whole once more. Board and glass lifted from the mess to mend themselves - returning to their prior state. Orange light filled the apartment, twinkling with power that zipped like static against Julia's skin when she touched it. Wood first. Then metal. Finally the glass, gleaming and clear to let the moonlight shimmer through.

Julia gasped. When he finished and met her eyes again, her lashes were wet with fresh tears but some of that softness had returned.

No reward had ever felt so sweet.

"Holy cripes…" Julia gulped. Honestly, she was hovering at the brink right at the moment but this… This helped so much more than she'd thought possible.

Her home was her sanctuary, cramped as it might be. Her emotions frayed - it had felt almost right that her place had been blasted all to shit just to mirror it - but as Thrynn slowly lowered his hands, his magic stroking her as it eased into the floor, walls and ceiling, she just couldn't stop herself.

It was like he'd pieced a part of her back together.

Half sobbing she barreled into his arms, leaping to wrap her legs around his waist like a spider monkey. When he stumbled, she buried her face in his throat and clung, drawing in his scent like life. She didn't give a damn if they fell – couldn't care less, really – but he managed. He chuckled and wrapped his arms around her, one hand bracing her ass so she could rest more comfortably against him.

"Hey now, it's alright-"

And she kissed him.

With all her heart and no little amount of desperation, she chucked good sense to the wind. Cupping his face in both her hands she pressed her lips to his, craving the fire and light, craving his taste. His groan thrilled her. And when his lips parted, when he surrendered, she'd never felt more like a woman.

This pleasure? It burned but it was sweet. It was thriving and brutal and *alive.* Gods, she needed to feel the touch of life with all this death and fear and frustration weighing the world down to Hell.

Power, heady and tantalizing, threaded through her. This male - this magical male who traipsed between worlds as though they were shops lining the streets, who repaired her home with nothing but a lift of a finger, who commanded the elements like a freaking kung-fu master - he shuddered beneath her fingers.

It was the hottest thing she'd ever seen.

Countless questions hovered between them. What was this? What would it become? What could it mean for her and the people in her life? What did it mean to him? But none of them mattered now, not while his hands braced her ass and his tongue taunted and teased.

Right now it was only them.

On a gasp she broke away, only to tear at his flannel until the buttons popped and scattered. The moment skin touched skin she purred, actually purred her satisfaction.

"Hold-" Thrynn winced, the beast within reared against his hesitation, reveling in her enthusiasm, in her need. "Hold, damn it. Just a second."

"Why?" Julia's chest heaved with her breath, he couldn't tear his eyes away.

"I just-" He gritted his teeth against the growl when she dipped in close to nip at his throat, soothing the little hurts with gentle laves of her tongue. "By the gods, you're going to kill me."

She giggled and did it again.

With the final vestige of his sanity, he propped her back against the kitchen table and sped two steps away, forcing his fang through his lip until he tasted blood. It did little to help. "Not like this," His voice cut with the strain, his fists clenching hard enough to hurt.

Her sultry smile faded as she watched him, "What? I don't

understand."

Hell, he wasn't certain he did either. Nostrils flaring, that mouth watering scent of her arousal blooming in the air, Thrynn squeezed his eyes closed, pinching the bridge of his nose with his fingers. "You're hurting, Julia. You're not thinking clearly."

It was as though the joy just sucked from the room with his words. He cursed, scrubbing his face with his hands before reaching for her again. Their skin flushed, their hearts pounded, but when he brushed his lips over hers it was soft.

"The first time I take you," Fang nicked her lip and he licked the tiny droplet of blood away, "It will only be you and me. You will surrender to me. Freely. Because you want me." He drew back, kissed the tip of her nose, "Because you trust me." Her cheeks, "Because you love me." Both eyes, "And I will gift you all that I am, all that I have in return."

With a final lingering kiss to her brow he released her. She flopped in a chair, staring at her trembling hands. His heart twisted to see that lost look on her face so he swiftly knelt before her. "Calm, my Julia. It's alright. You're safe, *mo chroi,*" But when he reached for her hand she tugged it from his grasp.

"I need to work." She shot to standing fast enough to knock the chair over and winced as the bang sent Rool skittering into her room, "Crap... I'm sorry." Her cheeks flushed scarlet as she tucked her hands safely in her pockets, "That was... Unfair."

Thrynn's eyes narrowed on her, "It was not."

But Julia was backing away. She felt dirty and sad... And embarrassed. Whatever this thing between them was, no matter how strong the pull or how delicious the taste, it deserved better than that. He'd been right to stop her. She'd been desperate for life, for freedom, for light - and Thrynn was all that and more, that's for sure - but it hadn't been *him* she'd wanted. It had been relief.

And that was unfair.

She'd never had more than a passing fling with the lovers she'd taken in the past, but she'd always respected them. They were people - whole, interesting, complex people who deserved to see and be seen for everything they brought to the table. She didn't *use* people. It just wasn't who she was.

But she had used Thrynn tonight.

They would come together, she knew it as surely as she knew her own name. It was only a matter of time with this fire between them. Hell, it may have even been written in the stars for how crazy it sounds. It was important, maybe even vital, and she wouldn't allow this darkness to dirty any part of it. Even indirectly.

Gods, when had she embraced this?

The bond tugged at her heart, pulsing with his arousal and his concern. Honest and raw. It went against anything she'd ever learned of his kind, but he'd been nothing but free with her. Over and over again he'd used his own power to protect her and her home, mending every hurt from her side to her hunger to her freaking wall. And he'd done all of it without once asking for anything in return.

Just like he'd helped her that first night all those years ago.

Anyone with any sense at all wouldn't buy it. Her Gran would probably box her ears the moment she found out Julia had even considered the bond - let alone accepted it. But that was just it. They couldn't *feel* him the way she could. They couldn't know that every time he smiled at her or laughed it was with the whole of him, lighting up her soul as well. Sure, he'd all but blackmailed her into accepting it - but even that felt unfair. Her soul had sung for him that day just as it did right now.

The simple truth?

She wanted him.

And that was... Oh man. That was a really big deal.

Standing swiftly she began to back towards her bedroom, towards safety. "I'm just gonna-" She threw a couple of thumbs over her shoulder like the dork she was, "Thank you for fixing the wall. No!" This was becoming a nasty little habit, but she was running low on options at the moment. When he rose to stop her she flung up her hands to ward him off, "Sorry, frick. I just need a bit, okay?"

Thrynn's jaw clenched, the thought of her even this far from him roused instincts he'd only ever encountered in combat before all this. But he'd seen. Even without the help of the bond, anyone attuned to her could read the realization on her face.

This anxiety was only natural.

She was finally learning that this – all of this – it meant real and total change for her. The emotions resonating through the bond, they weren't the feelings of a frightened wounded bird, or the shame and rage that colored her grief. They were the feelings of a woman, facing her man - facing her *mate* - and knowing that there was no turning back.

Though it pained him, he let her run. There were things he needed to do, things he needed to prepare so that this lost, heart-broken look never marred her beauty again.

The beast within raged.

But battle would have to be enough for now.

~Chapter Eighteen~

Meet the Murphys

October 22, 2021

The front door smashed open with a bang.

Thrynn startled so hard he damn near fell flat on his face before instinct kicked in. Before he'd even rubbed the sleep from his eyes he'd rolled to his feet, ancestral sword drawn and magic pulsing around him to assess the threat.

"Damn it all, Lass! Didn't I tell you to call us *immediately* if anything else happened? Oh-"

The little elder woman skidded to a halt half way to dump her things on the couch. Her eyes widened and after a long moment - he wasn't sure who had shocked the other more - a slow, wicked smile curved her lips. "Barren and dry, my ass."

"Gran!"

Julia slammed from her bedroom, took one look at Thrynn standing there half naked and brandishing a sword that looked like it could whoop anything from *Final Fantasy* and slapped her hands over her eyes, "Oh my god."

The colorful little elder only cackled.

It only took Thrynn a moment. He'd watched enough of Julia's life throughout the years to know who this was and why she didn't trigger the wards - and when Rool came padding out, wearing something akin to a little fluffy hound of some kind and rubbing the sleep from his eyes as though nothing were amiss? Thrynn was certain of it. This was Lillian ó Súilleabháin, and from what he could feel of it, the years had shaped her into a very accomplished mage in her own right... A particularly amusing one at that.

Relaxing enough to release his weapon back to Yvelta, Thrynn straightened and began to approach the little elder to grant her proper greeting. But Julia squeaked and flushed bright red.

"Oo Boyo," Gran whistled low, "I don't know what you did to land you in the doghouse but it must've been bad. Any woman would have to be dead or senseless not to jump all over that -"

"Gran!"

"- And I know my Jules isn't either of those."

When Julia just gaped at her, a mixture of horror and humor flooding the bond, Thrynn couldn't help but smirk along with the delightful little female's cackle. It was infectious after all.

"What are you even doing here? Cripes, it's barely sunrise!" She'd seen more of the dawn in the last few days than she had since her school years and the thought did *not* sit well with her. Julia took one look at Thrynn, narrowed her eyes and stabbed a finger in his direction, "Put some clothes on! For the love of god!"

"Which god?" Thrynn grinned when she squeaked again.

Gran sent him a wink, "Best do as she says, Boyo. Wouldn't want Eric popping a vessel at the sight of you-"

"Dad's here?"

"Your Ma, too."

"Oh, Hell." Julia scrubbed at her face until most of the pink had faded and stomped into the kitchen. If she was going to deal with this, she was going to need coffee. Lots of coffee. Gallons.

"Be a dear and throw some tea on for me, would you? These old bones aren't what they used to be."

Julia scoffed, "Work well enough, far as I can see."

As the women made their way to the kitchen, Thrynn cast his senses to the rest of the building. He wasn't sure what Julia was so embarrassed about - since when had a man's naked chest caused anyone such grief? But the worry was there and, though he found the whole thing rather amusing, the last thing he wished to do after last night would be to put his mate through any undue stress. Though she wore a steady facade, she couldn't hide from him. She was raw, tangled... Fragile. When he found the two souls, familiar to him though he'd never felt them personally, that were making their way up the stairs to the second floor, arms laden and hearts filled with concern, he jumped to do as Gran suggested.

Quickly, Thrynn pulled on his rumpled white t-shirt and jeans before calling up a minor glamour spell to smooth everything out enough to appear presentable. The flannel was draped over the arm of the couch where it would remain, still torn from Julia's attentions the night before. A trophy. Hard won and precious. There was little he could do to mask his nature - nor would he. It was with pride he claimed his little Human, and he had no intention of deceiving the family that loved her so dearly. So he made himself just decent enough not to frighten, and then followed instinct and went straight to Julia, trailing his fingers down her rigid spine.

When she sputtered and pulled away, his brow lifted.

"Answer the question, Gran."

"What? A freak lightening storm in the middle of a sunny day hovering specifically over our girl's building just after she's endured-"

"Touche," Julia muttered and scrubbed at her face again.

"Why didn't you call us? I knew, Mrs. Ricardo, you know. Went to Stitch & Bitch with her every Wednesday. So why in all blue Hell is it that I have to hear the news through the gossip line and not from my own flesh and blood?"

Julia just rolled her eyes.

Though she stiffened, Thrynn pressed a palm firmly to her back, ranging himself beside her, "We were attacked."

Julia slammed her elbow into his gut but he only squeezed her side, "Do not allow him to isolate you. Not from them. This is your power, Sweetheart. Separating you from them is exactly what he wants."

A loud crash at the door saved her from answering, but she'd already caught the speculative look in her Gran's eye. This boyo had suddenly become even more interesting, if that were possible.

"Careful! Don't tip it!"

"Christ, Woman." Eric grunted and then he and JoAnna circled the wall to enter the kitchen with the rest of them. He was hauling an over sized box, imbalanced and steaming from the top, "Couldn't just grab a box of donuts, oh no -"

"A donut is *not* a meal and-" JoAnna skidded to a stop the moment she saw Thrynn. "Oh my god."

Eric was still muttering.

Thrynn moved to help Eric slide the box of food onto the counter.

"Thanks, Babygirl. See? Glad you've still got your manners helping an old- What the fuck?"

Eric stumbled back. Ranging himself in front of his wife and her mother. He was a large man, always had been, but even he felt dwarfed. He was a working man, a farmer, and as he'd spent most of his free time over the years chasing his wife all over the wilderness, hunting up roots or berries or stones of power - whatever she needed or desired at the time - he was still plenty imposing. But this guy?

There was something off about this one.

"Jules." His tone held a note of warning and he never took his eyes off Thrynn.

For her part, Julia just chugged half her coffee.

In the way of his people, Thrynn pounded a fist to his chest, bowing slightly in greeting. "Lillian ó Súilleabháin, Grand Caster of the ó Súilleabháin line; JoAnna Murphy, gifted Empath and Seer; and you, Eric Murphy, beloved father and guardian of Julia's clan. It is honored I am to meet you all."

JoAnna made a sound somewhere between a whine and a prayer while Eric just stared.

Only her Gran had the balls to slap her knee like this was the funniest damn thing she'd seen in years, "Now that! That's respect right there, now in'it. I haven't heard a greeting like that since…" Her face fell as the realization hit her. Then all of them were just staring. Mouths open and gaping like a school of fish.

Thrynn's smile slipped a little so Julia finally came to the rescue, "Guys, it's fine. He's a friend."

JoAnna choked a little, "Julia, hush." She looked for all the world like she was ready to scoop her baby up and make a break for it down the street.

"Mama, seriously-"

"Jules." This from her father.

But Gran broke from them to round the corner and poke Thrynn in the side, "He's real."

Julia rolled her eyes.

"What in gods name have you done, Child?" Gran rounded on her with all the ferocity of a rainbow chihuahua. "Calling an Old God? Are you crazy? Everyone knows you can't trust the Fae-"

"Otherkin, if you will."

Everyone froze when Thrynn spoke.

"I can explain."

But Thrynn laid a comforting hand on her shoulder, "It's alright." When she turned to argue, he stroked a gentle finger down her cheek, "It's to be expected."

When he turned back to his mate's family, he did so with an understanding smile. "I assure you all, I mean no harm."

Gran ignored him rounding on Julia, "What did you promise him?"

"Nothing."

"Bull. You keep some strange friends, girl, but none I've seen swinging a sword like they knew how to use it. What did he ask of you? Did he give you anything? Touch you-" When Julia flushed, she roared, "You let him *touch* you?"

"Enough."

Gran snapped straight, her spine tightening about as hard as her teeth, he imagined. Though this elder charmed him thoroughly, Thrynn would allow no one to infer that anything between Julia and himself was something to be ashamed of. Nor would he allow anyone to place themselves between them - well meaning or otherwise.

"Enough," He said it gently this time, and though his hands remained on Julia's shoulders his eyes stayed steady on Gran until she finally deigned to meet his gaze. "'Tis obvious you know what I am. That means you know that my kind do not lie."

She actually glared at him, "Oh, you absolutely can! You just have to be more devious about it."

Thrynn smirked, it was almost word for word what his Julia had tossed his way during their first meeting. "Fair enough. Trust this then. There has never been a moment and there never will be, not in this life or the next, that I have meant Julia or her clan any harm. I am here because-"

"He's here to help." Julia finally stepped in. Her mother's coloring still hadn't returned and it was beginning to worry her, "Mama."

When her mom still didn't tear her gaze away from Thrynn to meet her eyes, she stomped her foot, "Mama. He's the one who sent Rude!"

That did it, "He what?"

At the sound of his name, the little Imp finally decided to enter the fray - however entertaining this little showdown had been. He hopped from the couch and, lifting his fluffy tail in the air like a shadow flag, came trolloping over to rub himself against her mothers' shins.

It was mostly instinct that had her crouching to give him a hug and a scratch, "Is this true?"

Rool dog-smiled and yipped.

JoAnna didn't know what to think. The Tuatha De, all the histories of her people swore up and down they weren't to be trusted, but the Fae came from a world as varied and complex as our own. They were complex creatures, capable of making choices and building relationships. She'd known from the moment her daughter had brought this little stray home after he'd saved her from the *Caol* that Rude was of that Otherworld. She'd known he was no ordinary creature. She'd just assumed he was a kind of spirit guide for her daughter - one that enjoyed a more hands-on approach. For twenty years, she'd trusted him with her most precious gift and not once had he let her down.

She saw no reason to stop that now, "Rude." She waited until the little Imp met her eyes and plopped his butt to the ground to show her he knew this was serious, "Are we safe? With him?"

Rool's head tilted, his eyes somber. Then he lifted a paw to place it in her hand and nodded definitively.

"Cernunnos."

Thrynn tilted his head, sending Julia a subtle shake of his head before she could speak. It wasn't that he wouldn't allow his kin to know his real name - when the time was right - but at the moment they were unsure of him and it was a dangerous thing. So he thumped his chest and bowed to her once more, "You may call me Cern."

Julia's brow furrowed but she obviously didn't want to rile them further.

Gran narrowed her eyes at him, scanning him up and down like a specimen on a slab. This one burned with a rare fire, that's certain. She would be a force to reckon with when nature called her home to the Otherworld. "You look pretty cleaned up for the Lord of the Wild Things, don't you? Where are your horns? We were promised horns."

Thrynn relaxed enough to allow his amusement to show fully, and as his face brightened much of the tension bled from the room. "I wear a glamour when I visit realms, unless and until I wish to be seen."

She waved expectantly, "Well?"

Julia sent him an apologetic look but he merely winked. He wouldn't show them his true form - he was near certain her father would snap if he did - but he could show them something.

Standing tall he closed his eyes, releasing the glamour just partially. His face sharpened, and as he lifted his hands to push back his curls, horns - shaped like the antlers of a grand elk but made of the hard, plated, black bone of his people - curved up and over his head, more majestic and intimidating than any crown.

The women gasped.

Julia bit her lip, eyes flaring.

Eric went dead pale.

The moment the man swayed, Thrynn reestablished the glamour. Catching the man's shoulder and shoving him firmly toward a chair at the table he said, "Relax, my friend. A little food and water will do you good."

The moment she saw her mate falter, JoAnna rushed to his side.

"He's put up with a helluva lot over the years, but it's different. In your face like that. It's different," Gran said, and if he wasn't mistaken there was a distinctly protective note to it.

"I understand completely. Come, Sweetheart, let's us prepare some food for your clan. Then we can decide our approach to this darkness."

JoAnna spoke up from her father's lap where he cradled her firmly against him for comfort. "There are biscuits-" She cleared her throat when Thrynn raised a brow in her direction, "There's breakfast there." She nodded at the steaming box. "Biscuits and gravy, plenty to share."

Because they all needed the routine of it, Julia set to preparing the food while Thrynn set the table. The Murphys watched him warily each time he moved, but as long minutes passed in the morning sun the tension slowly eased.

From her perch on her mate's lap, JoAnna studied him. "Mrs. Ricardo... This was a blatant attack."

Thrynn nodded, "Aye. He wished to impress her-" When Julia sucked in a breath, he went to her, soothing her with a touch, "And then he wished to force her hand. I don't believe he'd expected her to fight back..." He paused, bringing Julia firmly into his warmth because he could feel her distress and it tore at him. "But it is a battle he will get."

Gran slapped her hands together, "Then eat up! We've got

work to do."

Later, they all sat at the table, surrounding the second meal he would share with his new family: a couple of pizza pies that Thrynn had proudly procured. Though he enjoyed the concoction immensely, it was a sad mockery of what they deserved. In his own world he would have laid them a feast of fresh meats, veggies and fruits grown in his own territory and fetched by his own hand - but for now, this would have to do. They all were fairly receptive to the gesture regardless, and after hours of Crafting, testing the wards and reestablishing boundaries that may have been breached, everyone seemed to be just happy to rest, eat and plot.

"A united protection circle," JoAnna sipped at her tea while the rest fell silent, pausing with their pizza halfway to their lips. She was the kind that spoke rarely enough that when she did, even these guys would stop to listen. "Large enough to encompass the whole of Murkwood. With all of us here, we've got the power to do it."

"Not to sustain it though," Julia shut that down with another bite. "Something like that would take constant upkeep and we just don't have the manpower. And it's not like we can lock everyone inside. What happens when they leave to go shopping or something? I warded the entire building and it didn't do jack to help Mrs. Ricardo."

"That wasn't your fault." Eric moved to stand behind his daughter, stroking a hand down her hair in the way he had since the day she was born, "That's not on you."

He'd managed to pull himself together - Cern was right, a little food, water and the loving touch of his woman had done him plenty good - but all this still made him uneasy. It wasn't just that he felt totally outclassed as the only mundane Human here, though that was enough to give any honest man a heart attack, it was this.... Intensity between Julia and Cern. Never once in her life had his Jules allowed anyone to get so close, to be a part of this aspect of her life. Hell, the other guys hadn't even been allowed to speak with her family beyond the casual hello-goodbye decency wave. This was brand new territory - and the way Cern looked at his daughter? Any man would recognize that look in his eyes.

It was a declaration. A claiming.

There was nothing about it that seemed casual - and that begged a whole 'nother slew of questions. What did it mean? For her? For them? For their family? Would the old legends prove true? Would he try to steal her away? Because she definitely wouldn't go quietly. Not his Jules. No way.

Would he treat her with dignity? Respect? An equal partner in life as a modern woman should expect from the man she builds her home with? What of children?

It was enough to drive a sane man batty. But if he knew anything in this world it was that he could trust his daughter. She had solid judgment and a head stubborn as a mule when she'd set her mind to something. If this Old God thought he could push her around, Eric gave her a squeeze, it would be fun to watch her set him straight.

"A banishing then," Gran clapped her hands together, metal on metal clacking as her rings knocked together.

"Nay," Thrynn shook his head, sliding his hand onto Julia's knee to squeeze firmly. "Such a spell would require proximity and we have yet to even pinpoint the source. We'll need to draw him out." Julia flushed at his touch, but it was a good warmth that pulsed between them now, "All magic is tied to the Otherworld and the veil is thinning. Soon he will be at full strength."

Everyone went silent. Chilling.

"Sometimes," Thrynn murmured drawing Julia's attention to his somber eyes - fierce and feral, the eyes of a warrior, "The best defense is an offense."

But she was shaking her head, "We don't use magic that way. We have no idea how to-"

Thrynn hushed her with a firm shake of his head. "So innocent-" He pressed a gentle kiss to her brow, "So sweet. But

Julia, there are certain realities that must be faced - no matter how ugly they are."

She shoved at him, "Don't patronize me."

But Thrynn held firm, "This isn't something we can wait out. I've felt him - his intentions, his desire. He wants you, Julia. Not just your power or your body. He wants *you.* Any man could tell you that's not a passing thing." He and Eric shared a somber knowing look.

"I want him gone as much as anyone but that doesn't change the facts. We aren't waltzing into war here-"

"The cops." Eric shrugged a big shoulder and sighed into coffee that had long gone cold. "Not to sound like the muggle here," Julia rewarded him with a hesitant smirk at the reference, "but if what you say is true, this guy is still a guy. Witch or not. And he's close."

Julia scoffed, "And what exactly am I supposed to tell them? 'Hey guys, there's this dude that's got a serious boner for freaking me out. Remember the lightening storm that killed Mrs. Ricardo? He did that.' I'd be laughed out of the room."

Eric's jaw clenched, "Boone made Sheriff last election-"

"Boone Headly?" Julia asked, her brow tweaking. "Seriously?"

Boone Headly only had a few years on her but he was a decent dude. They'd gone to school together and he'd been at more than a few of the seances she'd had with her friends - mostly they were an excuse to gather around a fire in the woods and drink some cheap beer but still... He'd seen. And, at least back then, he'd believed.

"There's still not a lot they can do. This darkness - this man, whoever he is - he hasn't once used mundane tactics," Jo-Anna pointed out.

"But if he *is* a witch then he's still a guy. He lives here, pays rent, buys food, drives around, works. Having the cops looking for you - it's disruptive at the very least and a break in routine could be enough for us to find him." Eric rubbed at the sunburn on the back of his neck. He was so damn tired. He'd been tired before but never like this - like it was bone deep and terrifying because it was helplessness.

"It's a fair suggestion," Thrynn nodded to Eric. The two males seemed to consider each other for a moment, communicating something on some guy wavelength that went beyond the rest of them. And then Thrynn nodded again.

"If they're on alert, they'll be quicker to respond should we need them." Gran sighed, "But it's not enough. This darkness? It's pissed. There must be something more we can do-"

"I can bring my guard." Thrynn drew his free hand over his jaw, considering. It wasn't the resplendent troops that had served his father all those years ago, but the Otherworld contained beings that were mysteries even to him. His territory teemed with life, creatures loyal to him with power in their own right, creatures like Rool.

"No."

All eyes shot to Julia.

Her voice was low, controlled, "I'm the target. He's made that clear. I'm not willing to risk anyone else - Human or otherwise."

When he felt it Thrynn slammed to his feet, the cold surety flooding the bond iced him to his core. "I will *not* let you go to him."

"It's not your decision -"

"The Hell it's not! You're my mate."

The term echoed around the room, final and shocking.

JoAnna choked-

Gran looked for all the world like she couldn't decide whether to slap his hands away or hex him into oblivion.

Eric went still. Very, very still.

But Thrynn saw only Julia. All but snarling, he tugged Julia to stand before him, his hands cupping her jaw and lifting until she was forced to meet his eyes. "You are my mate." His words were measured, his eyes fierce. "My heart. I will not let you face him alone."

"Alone?" Gran roared, "Like Hell! You mess with one Murphy, you mess with them all."

"Agreed." Her father rolled his shoulders. The rest... Well, they'd face that hurdle when they came to it. So when his wife started to rise, her every instinct screaming to rip their little girl back to the nest where she could be safe and cared for, he laid a heavy hand on her arm. "Wait," When JoAnna turned incredulous eyes his way, he sighed and lowered his voice, "He's our best bet with this, and you know it."

"But-"

He hushed her with a firm shake of his head, "I won't risk her. We'll figure the rest out *after* this stalker is safely behind bars -" He raised his voice to address the rest of the room, "But we will figure it out."

Not that they were listening.

JoAnna nodded, barely intercepting Gran's dandelion barb before the thing could stab Thrynn dead in the ass - "Not now, Ma-"

"What do you mean-" Gran sputtered.

"One thing at a time." Far as he was concerned that would have to do. Tired or not, there was no way, in this world *or* the next, he'd allow his little girl face this all by herself. And Cern? Well, he certainly seemed to give a damn so that's something. An edge. An advantage.

Hell, maybe their only advantage.

Slapping his hands to his thighs as though that settled it, he rose. "I'm going to call Boone. We'll explain the situation. Even if there's not a lot he can formally do, he knows us. He won't laugh us off."

JoAnna was nodding too, "I'll prepare. We'll need talismans, obsidian and lavender..."

"You aren't listening to me-" Julia pulled as far back as Thrynn would allow.

JoAnna turned on her, "Yes we are."

"We're just not going along with stupid." Gran muttered, pissed as hell but cowed... At least for the moment. She drummed her fingers on the table and sent Julia a hard look.

“He's already killed once. Don't you get that? You can't just offer the town up on a platter to protect me.”

“Protect and serve - that's their job.” Eric was firm, “That's *our* job. We're your family, Jules. And you will respect that. You will respect *us*.”

Browbeaten, Julia slumped in Thrynn's hold, letting him pull her close, letting them take control. When he finally released her, she backed into the kitchen to pour herself a refill with trembling hands.

They’re terrified for her - Hell, she was terrified for herself - and they were hurting. She got that – it's not like she wouldn't have felt the exact same way had she been in their shoes. This plotting and planning - it helped. Even if it was mostly useless.

She’d decided.

It’s not that she wanted to die - not even a little bit - and, frankly, the thought of what other crazy shit this guy could have planned for her made the coffee slide down her throat thick as mud. But it didn’t matter.

One cannot outweigh the many.

Thrynn knew. She could see it in the way he watched her, even as her family all leaned in to argue and scheme. She could feel it - his own resolution - riding parallel to hers in the bond. But he waited.

They both did.

~Chapter Nineteen~

Together

Eventually the sun began to set and the others packed up to head home. "Boone's on alert. He's promised to ask around, call us if he sees anything suspicious. He wants a list of your past lovers, Jules, and friends. Whoever you think might have a thing for you, one way or another."

It'd be a short list, Julia thought, but she sent him a nod. "I'll e-mail him."

Gran poked at her, "Your mama and I are going to take a drive. See what we can see." She shrugged, "Maybe we can narrow the playing field a bit."

JoAnna nodded, though she remained quiet as she pressed her lips to her little girl's cheek. She'd touched her constantly throughout the day – to reassure Julia or herself, it didn't matter. It had helped even if it had felt a little sad.

"Come with us," Though he winced just a little Eric settled his hands on her shoulders, sandwiching her between them. "Both of you."

"Not tonight, Dad."

Not this night.

He heaved a sigh and pressed a kiss to her forehead, skimming his hands down to squeeze her fingers. "I don't like leaving you here like this."

"I will stay with her." Thrynn nodded to her father, dropping his hands to her shoulders and settling himself behind her.

Though she could tell he didn't like it, Eric nodded... And backed away.

"Take care of them, Dad."

He eyed her for a lingering moment and nodded, "With everything I am."

Then he ushered them out the door.

Thrynn held her still, even after the door slammed shut behind them and their footsteps faded down the hall. Already her Gran was on about one thing or another, and she could just see her parents rolling their eyes and squeezing close as they herded her toward the car.

Oh gods, if anything happened to them...

Dipping to whisper kisses along her throat Thrynn murmured, "I will not let you go alone."

Julia blew out a breath long breath, "I was hoping you'd say that."

She stood still and quiet, but he could feel the chaos roiling within. "Calm, Julia." Thrynn's massive hands wrapped her shoulders in warmth as he drew her close.

Her family were wonderfully loud, their presence a comforting distraction, but now that they had gone and the two of them were left alone, the void cut deep. As though he could sense it Thrynn called to the light. Candles of every color burst to life around them, casting her home in a warm, bolstering glow. The effect was like something from a fairy tale, lovely and romantic, and before she realized what he was doing he'd drawn her to the center of the room to sway.

"I need to work."

It had been really, really nice to hang out with her family today - they always gave her a boost when she was feeling empty - but it had also served as a stark reminder of just how much she stood to lose.

But Thrynn only shook his head and circled her.

It wasn't that she didn't want to stay. Gods, but every thread of her being felt so wrapped up in him it seemed ludicrous to consider pulling away. But she was needed.

"I need to work."

"Nay," Thrynn drew his nose slowly down the lovely column of her throat inhaling her scent and reveling in it. "You're safe, *mo chroi.*"

"It's not me I'm worried about." When his brow lifted she shoved at him a little harder, "Seriously, Thrynn. Someone died! These are my people." Exasperated, she tossed her hand to the windows while he kept her nestled close in his arms. "Good people. Simple people. People just trying to live their lives the best they can. They don't deserve this bullshit!"

Thrynn's jaw clenched but he finally released her.

"First Travis, now Mrs. Ricardo?" On a roll now, Julia began to pace. It was better, at least, than collapsing into a sobbing, heaving heap. "Whose next? Eddie from the grocery store? Miss Roberta from the post office?" She flopped to her couch, letting her head fall in her hands, "My mom? Dad?" Her voice cracked, "Gran?"

She tore at his heart, he ached for her in every way. It had been many, many seasons since he'd first seen death firsthand, but he remembered - even though his had been nowhere near so.... Gruesome. You always remember your first. And his Julia, she had a gentle soul. Needing to touch her, to comfort and distract, he lowered to a crouch before her, gently but firmly gripping her knees. "They will be safe, Julia. This I promise you."

She loosed a brittle sigh, "You can't promise that."

Because he could do nothing else, he settled beside her and pulled her into his lap, cradling her head to his chest. "No?" His brows lifted, he twined his fingers through hers before raising her knuckles to his lips.

"You couldn't save Mrs. Ricardo."

"We weren't prepared." Thrynn smoothed her hair, the browns and reds gleaming in the firelight like a sunset, "We didn't know how far he was willing to go. We do now." Brushing his lips across her brow, his heart was so wound through hers in the bond he wasn't sure if the pulse was hers or his own - and it didn't matter. In the end, if she hurt, he did. If she loved, he did. They were one and the same. "And things are different now."

"They are?" She sniffled.

"Aye," Over her eyelids now, the apple of her cheeks, the

tip of her nose. Her sweet breath mingled with his and he knew nothing had ever made him feel so alive. "You have me."

Finally, her eyes opened to meet his, the gold shimmering with a tenuous hope, "What do you want from me?"

"Everything," He whispered, his fingers trailing down her spine to ease the tension riding there. "I want you."

"You want to sleep with me?"

He barked out a surprised laugh, somehow - even right now in the midst of all these shadows - she could still make him smile. "Yes. Absolutely. Gods, yes. But that is only a small part of it."

She chewed on her lower lip. The sight rushed straight to his groin, so he gently raised his thumb to tug it free himself.

"Then what? Why are you here? You called me your mate." Frustrated, she pushed to standing. "None of this makes any sense! I'm just a mortal, why would you give half a crap whether or not some psycho-stalker has his way with me?"

All humor fled as he stood, gripping her hips in his hands to pull her flush against him, "He will never touch you." The very thought was intolerable.

Julia gulped. She'd never heard him sound quite so… Inhuman before.

"You feel it too. I know you do."

The pull? The tug? "I don't know what you're talking about."

"There's a reason you came to me when you were but a child. A reason you fell into *my* den. Of all the shadows and corners of the Otherworld, it was to me you were called."

Julia's brow furrowed.

"Since that day, I've known. I recognized you. I didn't understand it, and I didn't know what it would become. But since that day you have belonged to me."

She shook her head as if to deny him, fear and a brutal lovely thrill flaring in her eyes, but he gripped her chin.

"As I have belonged to you."

It was clear as the written word, reading her face. She

struggled with it, the enormity of it, so he fed her each and every one of his intentions through the bond.

He was done waiting.

This darkness may have been the catalyst, but this - this wondrous spark between them - it was written in the stars. The Calling reaped its harvest on his soul and he threw himself into it with grateful abandon. Of all his travels, all his treasures, all his friends and lovers over the years - this night he would treasure above all others. It would rip them apart, piece by piece until they would be little more than chaos and need - and then it would rebuild them. A unit. A singularity. Never again would there be a Thrynn, lone wanderer of the far realms - and Julia, mistress mage and beloved daughter.

They would be as one.

Julia gasped, her eyes darkening with her power as she trembled in his arms. Accepting this, accepting him - it would mean irrevocable change. They stood, perched on a precipice more daunting than any towering cliff in that hellish dreamscape, and he knew it frightened her.

Hell, it frightened him.

Nerves riled the beast within to a frenzy as he trembled, her hips in his hands, her scent on his skin. Yet he waited.

In this, he would only accept total surrender.

"My Julia," He snarled it, fangs lengthening with his need.

Then, with a courage he could only marvel, she simply nodded.

Blessed release.

Simultaneously their magic burst from them, eager to stroke and dance and tease until there was nothing but color and madness.

And her.

She was everywhere. She threw herself to the passion with open eyes and an open heart - so vulnerable, so honest, so lovely and so brave. He vowed to them both that he would ensure she remain that way. Her body bowed - a perfect fit. The silky strands of her hair caressed his fists as her head fell back on a gentle cry. She bared her throat to him, a goddess in cotton and gold.

And he would revel in the worship of her.

With a low growl she felt straight to her soul, he slicked his tongue up her throat. "I claim you this night, Julia Marie."

When she did nothing but gasp, his grip tightened. "Accept me. Say it."

She groaned. God, nothing had ever felt as good as he did in this moment. Chocolate? Music? Hell, her Gran's world famous cream pie? Nothing could compare. Desire, biting and damn near hot enough to burn, drove any sanity that remained from her mind.

"Say it now."

All she wanted was him.

Her soul all but stood up to dance at the realization. It felt so right. So absolutely *right.* Twenty days or twenty years, it didn't matter when the will of the gods read clear as day in all that she was.

With a ripping cry the choice was made. Her head whipped up and she cupped his face in her hands, forcing him away from her throat so that she could meet his eyes. He snarled but she didn't fear him, his desperation only mirrored her own.

"I accept your claim, Thrynn, and make a claim of my own." She pressed her brow to his as he heaved against her, "You are *mine.*"

He roared his triumph, the wilds ripping through him to tear his facade to shreds. Horns rose majestic from his brow, his body glowing as his wings - auburn as his hair, feathered and feral - tore from his spine to frame him. Even his face had changed, just slightly, sharpening just enough to seem more wild and all the more gorgeous with it. His fangs lengthened until they near pierced his skin.

An instant of terror - what if she ran from him? What if he scared her?

"You're beautiful," She murmured her wide eyes hot and her touch gentle.

And the rage in his eyes softened a moment before he swept her into his arms and carried her to bed, "As are you, *mo chroi.*"

"What does that mean?" She gasped, clutching his horns for balance.

Reverently, he laid her back upon the sheets, white and rumpled from the night before, "My heart. Beloved." Her scent was everywhere here, fresh and sweet, soothing his mind even as it riled his spirit to delirium. Still he was soft, her surrender a gift he would cherish all his days and one he would accept not with desperation but with tenderness. Following her down, settling his weight between her long, creamy thighs, he dipped his head to taste her.

She melted.

His flavor burst over her lips, intoxicating and delicious. She trembled beneath his hands as he trailed them down her sides, then back up, the cotton of her shirt lifting to bare rosy skin until she was left in nothing but simple black underthings. One day he would drape her in silks and lace, but even then none would compare to this first time.

He cherished her.

Tossing the shirt aside, he brought his chest flush to hers and swallowed her groan. They held.

A beat.

Another.

And she went wild beneath him. Tearing at the remnants of his clothes until she could taste every inch of him, his throaty groans only encouraging her as their dance continued. She shoved at him until he leaned back on his knees, his wings spread wide behind him, cock straining for her. Monster and angel wrapped into one.

She purred, that addictive power from before coursing through her at the sight. This male - this *god* – waiting, trembling with need for her. She basked in it. And, with a playful grin, leaned in to take him into her mouth.

Sheets shrieked as his claws ripped through them at her

sides, "Julia..." His breath hitched when she sucked, "By the gods." Her eyes glinted as she smiled around him, her golden magic weaving up to tease at his sensitive wings. Unable to help himself he rose, gripping her hair in one clawed hand to pull her deeper.

He took control - with anyone else it would have pissed her off, but... She'd never trusted anyone this way before. If you could even call it trust - it was more of a *knowing.* An absolute surety that there was nothing he would do to harm her, even as he pushed her, even like this.

He thrust into her throat, her little whimpers and moans driving his own until he nearly spilled, right then and there. "Not like this," He gasped it, pulling her from him by her hair and rolling with her until she was splayed, her arousal perfuming the air. When he kissed her again, he tasted himself on her lips - so satisfying.

"My turn," He growled it while she gasped, lowering himself inch by inch, nipping and sipping at every lovely dip and valley of her. At her sides his claws tore through the flimsy fabric of her chest piece, and she was glorious. So small and soft, so loving and bright, he sucked her nipple between his teeth and rolled it until he had her writhing with want beneath him. So receptive.

Her pleasure thrummed within him, tangling with his own until they were lost in it. The edge lingered just beyond, and he was desperate to watch her fall, to bear witness to every expression as ecstasy sent her flying by his hand.

Only ever by his hand alone.

"Thrynn please, I need-"

"I know what you need." He growled it, scraping his fangs down her stomach to the final barrier, "Your wants, your needs, your darkest secrets - they belong to me."

With that growling declaration he took her panties between his teeth and ripped them away, grinning when she gasped and arched beneath him.

"Cripes, please!"

Out of her mind, totally lost in this storm of satisfaction

and yearning, all she could think was that she needed. Him.

Then his mouth was on her and there was nothing else. Fuck! That tingle that followed anywhere his tongue touched her felt like straight magic on her now, as he laved her slit from bottom to top. "So fucking sweet…"

And then he feasted.

While her body throbbed and pleasure overwhelmed her, his touch was so deliberate, so precise - a port in the storm. He played her perfectly, like a master pianist, her shuddering moans a symphony of love. Because that's what this was.

Love.

The thought sent her flying.

Thrynn watched her go, hands sliding up her sides to link with hers as she threw her head back and arched into him. His teeth and tongue drawing out the orgasm until there was nothing left to give.

Then he returned to her.

"Holy crap…" She gasped.

"Stunning."

He grinned and nuzzled at her, enjoying the languid way she settled against him even as her hips moved of their own accord to seek him out. Instinct, hers and his, calling him home. But he was large, even for a female of his own kind, and she was Human - slight and soft at that. He didn't want to hurt her - he couldn't live with himself if anything -

"Now," Rousing through the fog of bliss just enough to wrap her arms around his neck, Julia rose to nip at his jaw. "Please, Thrynn. I need you now."

He could deny her nothing.

"This…" He choked as she sucked at his lower lip, "This won't be easy for you." He caught her wrists, pinning them above her, drawing himself against her core, "It will hurt you." Before she could say anything he moved against her again, dropping low so that his lips hovered just above her own, "But it will get better, I promise."

Julia shuddered, everything about him was huge - his

aura, his personality... Everything. There would be pain - she was sure of it, her body clenched at the thought - but his eyes promised pleasure beyond her wildest dreams. She could deal - her breath caught as he carefully slid a thick clawed finger inside her, rocking her, stretching her.

His jaw clenched, his eyes flashed.

She was tight - so freaking tight - and they'd barely just begun. But she would take him - they were meant. When he added another finger she reared up, crying out and damn near dislodging the hand that pinned her wrists to the bed. "Easy! Easy now. I've got you." Trailing his tongue over her throat he calmed her, "I've got you, Sweetheart."

Oh fuck. Even this moved her like nothing before. He played her, working them into a gentle rhythm so tender and perfectly opposed to the wicked claws within her pressing always just to the brink of pain. It was intoxicating. Addicting. If she moved just the wrong way he would tear her but that only thrilled her more. Whimpering she lifted her hips, wordlessly offering all that she was.

"Calm," Thrynn murmured, pressing one more inside.

It burned, but it wasn't anywhere near his size.

"Relax, Julia." Thrynn thrust knuckle deep and held, forcing her to feel him, to adjust. "Trust me."

"I do."

It was the truth. She did trust him. She loved the feel of him over her, inside her - even if it hurt. She wanted this.

She relaxed, the moment she did the burning eased into an intense warmth, but it felt good. So freaking good.

"One more," Thrynn gritted his teeth. She was a dream, wet and ready for him, but he wanted to be sure. She needed to know how good it could be before-

"Cum for me, Julia. Now."

She flew.

Her spine arched into him as he withdrew and settled above her. Their magic sparkled and throbbed in time with their pounding hearts as he settled himself against her.

As he pressed.

Pain pierced the veil - unexpected and brutal.

She tensed, instinct had her attempting to pull away but with one hand on her shoulder, another on her hip, he held her steady. "Only a moment. I swear. Only for a moment," He gritted. His fangs fully unsheathed now.

Gods but it hurt, it was almost too much - but she forced herself to remember how wonderful he had made her feel just moments before. He was there, straining. And she was safe. His scent engulfed her, and somehow that made it a little easier to take. She drew greedy breaths as he slid deeper inside, "Fuck."

"I've got you."

But Julia surprised him. Though tears spilled from her eyes, she didn't retreat from him. Instead she wrapped her arms around his neck and clung as he eased them into a slow rhythm.

"Thrynn," She gasped.

"I know," He kissed her, "It will get better."

"So good..."

He jerked in surprise at her words, causing her to bite down hard on his throat to stifle her cry. "Julia?"

"Don't stop." Julia lifted her hips rocking into him.

Pain and pleasure were one and the same now – but it was *delicious*. He'd taken her - owned her completely - and she fucking craved more of it.

Thrynn couldn't believe it. This bliss - wet and hot and wonderful - it was a gift of the gods. She panted beneath him, ripping his soul from his body and into her own with every breath, and he fucking adored it.

He let go.

Losing himself in her - it was madness. Wondrous madness. He thrust into her, his wings beating to drive him harder, faster, deeper. And she met him fury for fury.

When she clenched on him, her core gripping him hard enough to hurt, he roared his joy to the moonlight.

Then sank his fangs deep into her throat.

Julia gasped, this was sharp and new but every time he

drew on her neck, her core throbbed on him. It tossed her into another orgasm, this one just as brutal, just as resonating as the last and amplified by his own pleasure, his own triumph echoing through the bond. Until finally, he released her, drawing back just enough to rest his brow against hers.

Quiet.

Their eyes met. Their magic entwined and lowered to blanket them in color and light.

He raised a claw to his own throat and cut deep, "Drink of me. Complete the bond."

Julia watched a drop of dark blood bead and then slide down to his collar bone.

"Claim me," He growled.

So she did.

With a smile.

~Chapter Twenty~

The Game

<u>October 31, 2021</u>

Halloween.

Normally this would have been her favorite holiday. It had always seemed tailor made to celebrate her most favorite of things: spooky stuff, magic, the onward rolling of the Wheel of the Year and a celebration of the second seasonal harvest. Growing up, she'd felt about Halloween a bit how kids normally viewed summer break – it was the end of a long work cycle, so now there was finally the time to rest, relax and bask in the glory of accomplishment.

But none of that would be the case this year.

Julia had never been a warrior - sure, she'd played the occasional shooter or two, and she could admit that she enjoyed the giddy feeling that came when her inner nine-year-old saw something blow up on screen in a particularly satisfying fashion - but this? This was a whole different ball game. There was life at stake - real, thriving, loving, meaningful life - and whether this went well or straight to shit, by the end of it someone would be dead. Their choices gone. Their last chance spent. And that was a sad thing -

Even for the darkness.

She'd always been a firm believer that anger and rage were born of pain, and although his actions had crossed about every line in the book, she could still empathize with that. This whole situation was tragic. And although they would walk onto a battlefield they didn't create - the guilt was there.

Feeling it, Thrynn stopped scanning over the spells they'd

prepped and came back to her. Saying nothing, he simply framed her face in his hands, steadied her and laid his lips on hers. Quiet understanding flowed between them - but there was a firm resolve underlying it all. If he could have, he would have swept her into his world and been done with it - stalker be damned. He wanted to - Gods, but it was tempting - but her heart was soft and full of this place, and he couldn't bring himself to hurt her like that.

So he would free this town.

He would free her family.

And then she would follow him - free to love and free to face their future with all the open enthusiasm he could ask for.

The door slammed open.

Julia jumped about half a foot into the air but Thrynn only sighed. Subtlety it seemed, was a concept lost on the Murphy's.

"What the hell are you doing here?"

Gran lifted a brow and slapped her hands on her bony hips, "You have to ask?"

Julia turned her accusing stare on Thrynn, "You called them?"

But he lifted his hands and shook his head.

"Hey now, Babygirl. If you're going to spit your venom at least aim it at the people who earned it."

Julia just gaped as her dad led her mom through the door with a steady hand at her back.

Gran stomped up to her and jabbed her hard in the stomach, "Now you listen here, and you listen good. You are a member of this family. You can't honestly believe for one instant that we would let you waltz into this-"

"No. No, no. Absolutely flipping not!"

Thrynn's hands came down on her shoulders. The mounting panic eased just a little at his touch but it wasn't enough.

No , it wasn't fucking enough!

These three people meant more to her than anything in the world. They had power of their own - formidable power - but they were also this darkness' perfect target. It was like having three obvious weak spots on ready display for the asshole to jab at until she fell.

"Do you guys seriously not get it? This isn't some game!" Not that she had anything else to relate it to, but still. "This guy has *killed* people. Freaking dead. Gone. The end. Fin. You think I can take him on when I'm terrified he can get to you-"

"That's exactly why you need us-"

"We have no idea what he's capable of - what he's willing to do-"

"You can't just waltz on into this like some sacrificial virgin and assume-"

Julia and her Gran faced off in the little living room, all but nose to nose as they yelled at one another.

Thrynn winced a little when Eric slapped a hearty hand to his shoulder, "Come on, now. They'll be at this for a while. Let's get set up and see what's what."

"They do this a lot?"

Eric shook his head with a little smile, "Stick around long enough and you'll barely hear it anymore."

JoAnna, for her part, was already clearing the kitchen table and spreading out a map of Murkwood. "The energy is local. We've driven around the village twice a day this last week to see if we could root out any consistent outlier, and as of last night I've found three areas that seemed particularly negatively charged." She circled the graveyard, the hospital and Old Man Gregor's farm. "The hospital and the graveyard? Well, the source seems obvious there. It's not unusual for those to put off fairly charged auras on a typical day but the Gregor farm? That's weird."

Eric nodded, "Gregor's land lays adjacent to ours. He runs the place with his four sons and their wives. Family operation, close-knit. Plenty nice enough, and pretty well liked around town. Couldn't say how long they've held that land, but I know they've had it since I was a kid and probably longer than."

JoAnna straightened, "The focus there could mean that they're the next target... But it's a weird choice. If the point is to get Julia to come to him, why go after a family that's out of her general sight?"

Thrynn's jaw clenched and he shook his head, dragging his finger down the map. "This land runs alongside yours?"

Eric tilted his head, "Not exactly. I know what you're thinking. Maybe he set up there to target us and ours, right? But if that's his only objective the James' or Thompson's place would have been a better choice."

"Travis?" Evidently they'd come to a stalemate - which looked to mean that Julia had finally given up - as she, arms wrapped around herself to ward off the chill of fear, sidled up to his side. "He was a random target-"

"Wait a minute," Gran tapped a finger to her lips, "Where did you say he drove across the liminal edge?"

"Highway 77, heading East past-"

"Right alongside the Gregor Farm."

Julia's brow furrowed, "I've known the Gregor kids my entire life. They didn't have the gift - at least not anything strong enough that I could sense."

"They could have masked it," Thrynn murmured, "If they were strong enough and aware."

JoAnna just shook her head, "I don't know. I'm friendly with Gregor's wife Mary and I've been to their house countless times. I've never felt anything like that."

But Julia stared hard at the third circle on the map.

"What is it?" Thrynn nudged her until she cleared her throat and glanced around to see everyone staring at her.

"Sorry," She cleared her throat again, "There." She tapped her finger on the corn fields, "That's where I fell through... When I got Rude."

"A *Caol.*" JoAnna considered, "But aren't they random?"

Thrynn shrugged, "Nay. They're always there, but sometimes..." He tilted his head trying to come up with the best term for it, "They're more... Distanced? The realms are not stationary, they shift and sway with space and time as it stretches and bends."

"Like leaves on a tree in the wind," Julia murmured.

"Precisely." Thrynn grinned, "The veil is at it's thinnest tonight - the bridge between this world and my own at the closest point in their arc. But it's a gradual thing."

"Which means that the link to Otherworld magic increases over time," JoAnna sighed.

Julia nodded, "It's probably why he started with the dreams. It's the easiest breach... Then, because I was difficult, his frustration grew and that intensified his intent-"

"It would explain his odd lack of control," Thrynn tilted his head, considering. "I'd thought that any who could access the level of magic he was using had to be an accomplished mage - but a natural born, gifted in calls to the elements who was so emotionally charged? It's possible."

"He's going to do something tonight." Eric shrugged when everyonc turned his way, "The veil's at it's thinnest tonight, right? We have to assume he's aware."

Thrynn nodded slowly, his eyes darkening with a wicked solemnity, "Tonight it is."

Julia cursed, "But we aren't ready. There's no way we'll be able to place the protection charms in time. We can't risk the fall out-"

"Maybe not the whole town," JoAnna tapped the map, "But we can contain this."

Gran grinned, "We pick the place, we pick the time. This time the bastard is playing *our* game."

"So," Thrynn braced, the beast within rearing at the prospect of battle to come even as he brought his hand to Julia's stiff spine, "We bring the game to him."

~Chapter Twenty One~

Heirloom

Julia lingered at the window – just as she had most of the day. The sun had risen, rounded her and slowly began it's descent while the residents of Murkwood turned out in storm to celebrate. Pumpkins and webbing, spooky skeletons and plastic cauldrons full of smoking dry ice pumped layers of fun into the street where pirates and zombies mingled with princesses and fairies like they were the best of friends. She'd bought candy for them – despite the fact her home was in an apartment building, kids flocked here to see their own resident witch turn a trick or two – but this year the glass skull bowl remained tucked in her cupboard.

She couldn't risk it.

Warm, heavy hands landed on her waist, drawing her back flush against Thrynn's heat. He nuzzled her, then rested his chin atop her head to scan the streets himself. “Charming, isn't it?” When she shrugged he mustered a chuckle for her, “I always found Samhain to be one of the more amusing Human celebrations.”

“I thought it was meant to spook evil spirits-”

He squeezed her until she squeaked, glad to hear her try for humor even now. “And so it does, Little One. In fact,” He nuzzled at her neck, “I find myself thoroughly in need of comfort. Perhaps something warm... Wet...” He nipped at her, “And very, very distracting.”

“Halloween's always been her favorite. Isn't that right, Jules?” Utterly oblivious, Gran poked her in the stomach and cricked her neck like a boxer. “We're headed out. The sun's going to set here at..." She glanced at her phone to make sure, "About half past seven. It should be enough time to set the circle and ready ourselves. Make sure to eat something, you hear? Something decent, meat and potatoes like. You'll need the energy."

Thrynn nodded, "Alright then. We'll meet you at dusk."

"I don't like it," Eric stood, hands on hips and brow deeply furrowed as he scanned the map, the heap of spell pouches and the talismans all of them would wear come time. "This plan leaves way too much to chance. We're working on assumption-"

"No," JoAnna sighed, guilt and fear mixed in her wide eyes when she looked at them, "He'll be there. I scanned this town over and over again the past couple of weeks, there's not another place in a thirty mile radius that had the consistent energy signature that Gregor's did-"

But Eric was shaking his head, "Even so. Bringing a fight to *his* door? We have no idea what tricks he might have up his sleeve-"

"We know his intention," Thrynn murmured.

"And he knows ours. Hell, he's been using it against us this whole time. What if he's got the good sense to hide? Distance works the same both ways. His power might be the strongest tonight but what if he thinks it would be too obvious? What if he decides to wait until tomorrow when his strength is just as-"

"He'll come."

Julia said it quietly but everyone turned to her, "All he's asked for this entire time is for me to come to him. If I show up there, even if he's hiding, he'll show."

"Bait," Eric spat. "You're not bait, Jules! You're my daughter-"

"Dad." She headed straight into his arms. Burrowed deep.

"You're my daughter, Jules." His hands trembled as they wrapped around her, his breath shuddered, "I don't know how to protect you from something like this."

"Lucky for me, you raised me to protect myself then. Huh?"

He sputtered, "From a school yard bully! Not some obsessive, crazed witch of the Netherworld."

"She will not stand alone," Thrynn stated firmly.

Her Mama and her Gran nodded too, "We'll be right there-"

"And you hold more power than you think, Eric Murphy." Thrynn gripped his shoulder, soldier to soldier. "You've a strong heart. A steadfast soul. You've done more to defend your home and your kin throughout these years than even you realize. There is not another I would choose to walk into this battle by my side."

Her Mama rose to come to her mate, her touch seemed to steady him before she held out a talisman Julia had never seen before, "Take this."

The amulet swung from her fingers, heavy and ornate. A silver circle, worked into leafy vines and sectioned subtly to reflect the seasons, framed a lovely golden jewel, raw and wild and pulsing. The moment her skin brushed it, the jewel lit from within, a tiny flame that warmed the stone just barely, "What is this?"

"An old family heirloom." Her Gran stroked a thoughtful finger down it, "One that has lived in our line for generations. My mother granted it to me on my wedding day and I haven't had the heart to part with it since."

"I've never seen you wear it," Julia frowned.

"Some things are too precious to share."

Julia bit her lip. She knew the look in her Gran's eye. It was the look she always wore when she thought of her Patrick, and it tugged at her heart. "Are you sure, Gran?"

Gran nodded taking the chain herself and, with a whip of her magic, linking it at her throat so that the jewel hung heavy to her heart. "Aye," Her eyes twinkled gold, "Looks beautiful on you."

"Thank you." Julia touched it, already she could feel the strength of her family flowing through almost as direct as the bond-link.

Her Mama cupped her cheeks in her hands, lifting her eyes to hers. "We will be with you every step of the way. I swear it."

Julia gripped her wrists and kissed her cheek, “I know.”

Her dad swept her up into a bear hug, squeezing tight, “I still don't like it.”

She snorted and kissed him too, “I know. I love you.”

“Love you too, Babygirl.”

“Well, we'd better head out.” Gran clapped and her rings slapped together in a hard metal clack. “We need to set up before the veil reaches peak.”

Julia stepped back, her hand reaching for Thrynn's as she forced herself to nod. “I love you. Whatever happens, know that I always have and always will.”

Thrynn squeezed her fingers, “I'll keep her safe. You've my word.”

In a swirl of color and energy already snapping with power, they were suddenly alone.

There weren't words – they were unnecessary as the bond flowed hot and fevered between them. There was fear and resolve, anger and sorrow, but there was an almost frantic element to it. A foreign brutality. A raging possessiveness. When he slammed his lips to hers, she opened to it-

To him.

They'd come together in so many ways over the past week – and each had rocked her so thoroughly it had branded itself onto her soul. Fast and hard, soft and slow. Sometimes laughing, sometimes dancing, and sometimes it was almost dangerous. But none had ever felt like this. This was feverish and final.

And she knew.

Maybe it was the first time she'd realized, really realized, that she may not live to see the morning sun.

So she threw herself into him. Cloth shredded under her panic, teeth scraped and bit with none of the skill or subtlety he deserved. But he met her – force for force.

When he lifted her, slamming her spine to the window and spreading her wide for him, his eyes were wild for her.

She barely had the sanity to question, “But what if-”

“Let them see,” He growled, his fangs lengthening before

her gaze. "Let all of them know that you belong to *me*." And he thrust inside – hard.

She screamed. She was soaked for him, but he hadn't prepared her and it hurt. Gritting her teeth, she snarled into his face as he gripped her shoulders pulling her down, deeper onto his cock. It burned.

It was brilliant.

Her nails dug deep into his shoulders, drawing blood even as he started into a painful, unmerciful rhythm. But that was perfect. She didn't want mercy – softness would hurt more than this. And this? It was fucking delicious.

His glamour ripped from him as he lost himself, his wings tearing from his back, his horns rising from his brow, wicked and pointed.

She owned him.

She would show this darkness – she would show the world. Gripping his horns, she used them for leverage, wresting control and riding him into a blissful frenzy.

When he roared, when he slammed a clawed hand to the window beside her hard enough to crack the glass, when she felt him pulse deep within her, filling her, claiming her – she felt like a queen.

And feeling it – she flew.

~Chapter Twenty Two~

All Hallows Eve

It was surreal – standing here, Thrynn at her side and Rool in his natural visage riding her like a demented backpack.

The sun barely touched the horizon, an explosion of color and finality. As they had that first year and every year after that, the Gregor Farm had taken Halloween to heart and lined their land with all the favorite trappings. Spooky booths dotted the lawn offering everything from face-painting to caramel apples and, just as it had when she'd been seven years old and bratty with it, a signpost had been pounded into the soil to signal the start of the corn maze. The stalks didn't seem so tall anymore, not half as daunting as they had been that day, but they still towered over them as they swayed in a wind not born of the clear sky.

"Thrynn," She murmured, smiling as genuinely as she could when a couple kids waiting in line pointed at her and shrieked.

"Look! Mommy, look! It's the witch!" The little girl had big, sweetly rounded eyes all decorated with glitter and charms. Her little witch hat nearly fell off her head as she bounced on the balls of her feet, tugging at her mother's dress until the woman sent Julia an exasperated smile.

Julia grinned and crouched, "Me? Looks to me like you're the little witch here."

The girl scanned her and screwed up her face, "Why aren't you wearing your hat? Don't you know?" When she leaned in close to stage whisper, Julia leaned in to hear, "The veil is thin tonight!"

Julia's face fell. Something about the tone, the choice of words – it was... "Oh, yeah? Where'd you hear that?"

The girl's eyes flashed violet, so brief she could almost believe she imagined it. Julia dropped the little hand she'd held like it burned but the little girl only giggled sweetly, "He's waiting for you, you know."

Julia didn't respond.

"He saw you."

Julia just shook her head, "What do you mean?"

"He says to tell you, 'Happy Halloween!'"

She sucked in a sharp breath, it couldn't be...

The mother gripped her little girl's shoulder, her eyes flashing that same violet for an instant, "Come on, Ginny. Miss Julia's got somewhere to be." She hesitated, "Somewhere important."

But the little girl turned to Thrynn, sticking her tongue out. "Better not bring him though..." She let her Mommy draw her away, but turned back. "Wouldn't want something bad to happen."

Julia gulped, but she didn't rise. A moment passed, only a moment, but when the girl turned back to her mother she was all toddler giggles and smiles again as though nothing had happened.

"Puppets," Thrynn muttered, reaching down to help Julia to her feet.

She swallowed hard, fighting to clear a throat gone bone dry, "He was here. That day – the first time I fell through."

Thrynn's jaw worked but he only sent her a firm nod, scanning the crowd warily. "It doesn't matter. Not anymore."

"He knows we're here. He knows why."

Thrynn nodded, "We always knew he would, remember?"

She did. They'd been banking on it, in fact. But seeing it had shaken her. Thoroughly.

"We need to get them safe." She stared after that poor little girl. That sweet and innocent little girl. "We need to get them to leave."

Thrynn nodded, “On it.”

Closing his eyes, he opened himself. The Otherworld pulsed, the *Caol* thin and wispy. He called to Yvelta, drawing directly on the strength of his ancestors this day, then he raised his arms.

Clouds, thick and tumbling darkened the sun-shot sky, hanging low and oppressive even as the wind kicked into high gear. Storm magic wasn't his specialty, but he needed something quick and effective that wouldn't cause too much damage. It was risky – this male seemed to favor this element – but this was a small area and Thrynn had centuries of training and control on his side.

People paused, parents and kids alike, but none of them looked at him. They watched the sky with wary eyes, hovering at that brink. Kansans were used to storms, mostly they weathered them with a shrug and a grumble as they waited for the winds to shove on by. They were a hardy sort.

“It's going to take more than that,” Julia nudged Thrynn.

He nodded, and the clouds began to stretch and swirl.

Sirens blasted.

Everyone scrambled. The Gregors started ushering everyone towards their storm shelter.

And in the chaos, Julia, Thrynn and Rool slipped beyond the corn.

The instant Thrynn stepped beyond the line, the darkness ripped into a frenzy.

“Not so hard!”

“It's not-” Thrynn cursed. Never before had someone wrested control from him so quickly or so thoroughly. , "It's not me!”

Murkwood shuddered under the onslaught, trees shrieked their pain as they bent and swayed in the unnatural wind. The clouds turned black and violet as rain pelted soil, so loud and so fast it all but roared as Julia and Thrynn fought their way through. In all her years working these plains, she’d never seen such a storm. In an instant Thrynn's controlled threat had become brutality embodied, chaos and rage twisting together in a way Mother Nature would never have matched.

This was it.

She was sure of it.

Whatever the outcome, it all ends right here.

Thrynn gritted his teeth and raised his hands, drawing the shadows of the night around them to make a barrier. It wasn't enough, not hardly, but it cut through the cacophony so that they could speak. "I sense him."

Julia nodded, fingering the talisman draped around her neck and sending a brief prayer to her ancestors for aid. She could feel her family's circle like a small spot of constant warmth in her belly as they willed their support her way. She found comfort in it, but hoped with all her might they would heed her warning and get the hell out of dodge the moment this thing turned. This was wild magic, barely controlled. The darkness was losing his grip on reality in his desperation and greed.

"He's almost lost it."

Thrynn nodded, his face grim.

"What happens when he does?"

His jaw clenched as he glared at the storm, every inch the wandering warrior he'd claimed to be. Standing tall, he shed his glamour. Wings unfurled, mighty and beautiful even as the wind ripped at their feathers. Shadows swirled around him, hardening to obsidian as they formed into breathtaking armor that glinted as wickedly as the horns crowning his head. It molded to his form, the honored symbols of his Clan glowing with his energy where they'd been etched into the gleaming plates and resonating with an ancient, unknowable power. "Energy cannot be destroyed," He murmured and his eyes flared with his magic as the great sword *Neamhaí* manifested along his spine.

Blessed would be their battle this night, as the gods of Earth and Otherkin witnessed their struggle.

Julia's heart dropped. No, that's right. Energy can only be disbursed. Should the darkness lose control entirely, this storm he'd called would be unleashed on her home. She watched in mounting horror as black clouds lowered, swirling in a horrible mockery of a tornado. Nothing could survive this. This was beyond even the most seasoned Kansans ability. If they couldn't stop this here and now, Murkwood wouldn't be the only town lost to this madness.

"What do we do?"

Thrynn considered his little mortal. Already his essence had taken root, her eyes shone with it even in her fear. She was so strong, her soul pulsing with the love she felt for this place, her people... For him.

He knew.

Though she'd never given the feeling a voice – he knew.

And nothing in all his millenia of travels had ever touched him so.

"We use it." He waited until her glistening eyes met his, then trailed a gentle claw down her cheek, "We kill the bastard with his own sword."

She flinched at the mention of death but quickly caught his hand, twining her fingers through his own. With a solemn nod, she braced herself, "Alright."

"Or..." Thrynn studied her for a long moment, Rool pressing in against her knee, "I can take you from here. Right now. You can walk the worlds with me, travel the stars. This asshole be damned."

Her breath caught, it was all she'd hoped for but delivered at possibly the worst time ever. "Truly?"

Thrynn raised their twined fingers to his lips, pressing his promise there, "Aye."

"Then tell me the same thing after we take care of this asshat." With that she turned on her heel and stalked into hell.

As he had so many times in her presence, though the sensation was still a novelty to him, Thrynn laughed. This was his woman, indeed. Head held high and fire in her veins, he could ask for nothing more in this or any other universe.

"Shall we then?" He gestured to Rool whose fang glinted in

the strange light as his cowardice warred with his affection for the lass. Finally the little beastie nodded gravely and bounded after her, flinching when the dark clouds shot through with a horrible violet lightening.

Julia closed her eyes and opened her arms, casting her senses to the edge of the farm where her essence tied to her family. Each stood ready at the North, West and Eastern gates, waiting for her signal to lift the barrier.

"Be ready!" Her voice whipped away on the wind but Thrynn nodded as though he could hear every word, "The moment we do this he's going to freak!"

Rool slipped to her and crawled up her back like a monkey to perch on her shoulder, giving her a solemn nod to mirror his master's.

Drawing a deep bolstering breath she turned back to the fray.

Now!

A pulse of golden energy slammed into the soil, shooting straight to her family. Something shrieked it's fury - more animal than storm, but worse than any natural creature. It sounded like the realm bent around the sound of it, like Hell itself forced it free to rear up against them.

Julia...

The voice whispered in her mind, confident and seductive. The storm seemed to tighten, retreating into a swirling ball of energy within the barrier's walls.

Impressive, Little Witch, but then... You always have been, haven't you. He sounded... Proud. Of her.

"What do you want from me?"

The voice chuckled and it was warm and full, but it didn't reply. All sound was lost actually, almost as though the spiraling orb was sucking everything inside. It was strange. The air around her stilled and warmed even as the fields not two feet from her bent and groaned in it's fury. Even Rool clung to her, fangs bared in a tiny determined scowl as the wind did it's best to unseat him from her shoulders.

Still, she felt nothing.

Come.

The word sent an unholy shiver down her spine as memories reared, leaving her feeling small and violated.

I wish only to speak with you, lovely Julia Marie.

"You hurt people. My friends."

All I have ever desired was to speak to you.

"Well?" She waved her hand, "Start talking."

Thrynn watched her, wary and worried.

So he couldn't hear him. Figures, Julia winced and signaled to him to stay back. The voice sounded collected right now, but the energy still felt chaotic - on edge. And that stone weighing heavily in her stomach? It all but screamed that the moment Thrynn attempted to interfere, Murkwood would never be the same.

Not exactly... Intimate. Is it? This isn't what I'd imagined when I dreamed of our first meeting. Still, there's a certain poetry to it all.

"If you'd wanted poetry, you could have sent flowers."

As the Humans do? The voice almost chuckled, *Why lower ourselves to such base customs when we can shape the very skies to our will?*

"I am Human."

No... Forceful now, but still just as patient, *We're not. We're so much more than that.*

Suddenly the world shifted.

Gone were the tall, quaking stalks of Gregor's cornfield. Gone were the shining stars, the pulse of the Earth beneath her feet. Gone were Rool and Thrynn. She was alone.

And the cliffs were back.

Fuck!

Panic clawed - she couldn't feel her family. Crap, crap, crap! She couldn't feel Rool but he'd been on her shoulder only a second before. The bond shone from her heart but it felt lost, confused, tangled in the wind.

Shit!

"It's not real," She murmured it, but hell if it wasn't taking some work to convince herself. "It's not real." She couldn't afford to lose her shit right now, even if that line felt real damn close.

"Oh, it's very real. I can assure you."

She whipped around, her back to the raging sea crashing and groaning against the stones three hundred feet down. Her clothes were different too. Her pseudo-combat gear - which really amounted to a pair of black cargo pants tucked full of spell pouches, a stretchy black tank top and the brown pleather jacket her mom had bought her for Christmas last year - had been replaced with that same silky white dream gown, her feet left cold and bare against the rocks.

"This is Ardmore. Village of your forefathers, Young ó Súilleabháin, and soon it will be our home." He smiled gently, breathing deep of the briny air like it bolstered him. He gestured beyond him, to a little town nestled between rolling hills, forests and cliffs. A charming image, but nothing compared to the man.

Gods, he was gorgeous...

Too bad he was such a freaking tool.

This was the first time he'd allowed her to see him - but he was nothing like she'd expected. She'd been thinking typical monster-movie stalker - pale, maybe a bald spot, tubby with coke-bottle glasses... Always smelling like sweat and nerves. Robin Williams in *One Hour Photo.* This guy... He couldn't be more opposite.

He was perfect. Too perfect. Even Thrynn, minor god of the Otherworld, had smile lines at the corners of his eyes and freckles dotting his sun-kissed skin. This guy had none of that. He looked to be her age, but his skin looked as pale and flat as fresh off the press paper and his eyes shone the same startling violet as the lightening in his storms. He wore a skin tight black shirt and fitted jeans that left nothing to the imagination - and his physique fell somewhere between Olympic gymnast and hulking body builder. His hair lay pin straight to his waist, black but highlighted with what looked almost like the midnight blue of the starry sky, and it moved strangely when the sea breeze played at it - always precise, almost… painted.

He couldn't be real.

This was another illusion - detailed - but fake as her Gran's diamond earrings. It actually comforted her a little bit.

She could break this. Hell, Rool would slap her awake in no time, she was sure of it.

"Who are you?"

He smiled and it was soft, patient. Condescending.

"I am your destiny, Julia."

Her eyes narrowed, she very nearly snorted but it didn't feel like the smartest thing to mock this dude when she stood inches from a very sharp, very high ledge. She remembered all too well how it had felt to fall. "What if I don't believe in destiny?"

He didn't have the same issue apparently. He scoffed and began to slowly approach her, his expression calm and controlled but for the wild thrill in his eyes. "You know as well as I do the realities of things. Don't pretend to hide as the Humans do - not with me."

She edged around, hoping to get the forest at her back so that she could keep some distance between them. "What do you mean 'hide'?"

His smile turned feral when she circled him, "You wish to play?" A low growl rumbled in his chest, "I love to play." His eyes flashed as his power whipped out to wrap her in violet, sparking and burning where it gripped her skin.

While the shock of it had her gasping, he slipped his finger between her lips. It was cold. Even as he groaned and buried his face in her throat, his skin felt ice cold. "Soon," It sounded like a promise to himself more than anything else, "Soon, Lovely, but there are things to be dealt with first."

His tongue slicked up her neck and she shuddered with revulsion, "Fine." Anything to get his hands off her - *please god* - anything would do. Reeling back as far as she could in his grip, she turned her jaw from him, "No hiding, right?"

When he nuzzled her again she loosed her power - gold

coated her skin, shoving at violet until his hands and his essence were forced from her body. "Truth goes both ways. Take me home."

His eyes flashed but he didn't lash out, not the way it was obvious he wanted to. He looked ready to beat her bloody with his heaving shoulders and gritted teeth. "Stop being difficult," He snarled. "I've prepared so carefully – at least awaken enough to see the beauty I gift to you."

He side stepped, and at the wave of his hand it was as though she were flying. Her toes clung to rock even as her psyche was thrust beyond it all - land and sea, endless skies waited, endless potential. And it *was* beautiful. Perfect. Balanced and shaded and lovely.

Like that fucking painting.

"Take us back." Her vision returned, she side stepped when he reached for her again. Her amulet pulsed and her magic rose between them like a sunlit shield. *Keep it cool, Jules.* "Can't start a relationship founded on nothing but lies - everyone knows that."

That gave him pause, "You wish to start a relationship?" His head tilted as he considered.

Gods, he was weird. Like an alien wearing a Human suit that didn't fit quite right. "That's what you want, isn't it?"

He made a sound, his brow lifting.

"This isn't a lie, my Lovely. It's a promise." His tone lowered, the seduction back, "I can give you this beauty, this power - all you have to do is let me."

She gulped, the violet turned soft against her gold, stroking and tempting. She felt it in her skin. "Show me your true face."

His brow lifted, "This is my true face." He grinned arrogantly and gestured to himself, "All of this will be yours, you've only to say the word."

Bullshit.

"What word?" Maybe she could turn this - maybe they wouldn't have to fight. If he wanted consent, wanted surrender, that meant he still had some moral boundaries, right? That meant he could be reasoned with. Maybe there was hope -

"Beg for me." He bit his lip, and Julia barely suppressed the sneer. Leching wasn't a strong enough term. "I want to hear you whimper for me. I want to hear you scream."

Then again, maybe not.

Gripping the bond and praying that Thrynn could feel her, she gritted her teeth, "Never."

His facade slipped - just a tad. Just enough to have his eyes darkening, his skin turning gray. His energy squeezed at hers even as he sighed, "I knew it wouldn't be so easy."

Seeming to come to some conclusion, he rolled his shoulders back, "No matter. It's to be expected, really. You've been immersed in their lies for so long-"

Thrynn felt her.

Orange light shot through the bond, bleeding into her gold and encompassing her in his fire. It roared around her, all heat and light, but there was no pain.

The man stumbled back, gaping. Panic and rage warring over his features, "Impossible!"

Doubling in, Julia tucked into the bond drawing on Thrynn's essence until she stood tall and in control once more. "I'm done with the lies!"

"What is this?" He shrieked, his power tightening it's desperate hold on her even as he rammed his fists against her barrier, "What have you done?"

"Show me your true face!"

But he was gone.

Man melted into shadow -

And the storm tore through her shields once more.

Julia fell to her knees, instinct had her shielding her head as the wind raged above her, the dark clouds of the storm racing in frantic circles around her.

But there beneath her, deep within the webbing of the soil, she felt them.

She was back.

Her family was there. Thrynn was there. Rool was there.

She just needed to get to them.

Forcing herself to stand, she had to lean into the wind to keep her feet. This was no ordinary call to the elements - this wasn't nature at all.

As she watched in mounting horror, creatures - shifting shadows and shapes - wove in and out of the chaos, roaring and screeching.

And there - Thrynn fought them off like some kind of medieval angel, hovering three stories up, standing alone against the legions of Hell. His wings beat hard, fighting the wind while he moved with a grace born of constant practice, his sword whipping through skin and shadow like butter. He used the storm to his advantage at times, allowing the winds to rip him from their attack or to force his blade further, faster through the enemy. As she watched, dozens of things fell from the sky – half shadow, half being – bleeding and morphing.

He will die!

The voice screeched it, his infuriated roar echoing within the confines of her mind.

You will bear witness and then you will finally know! You will finally see!

Something leaped. A creature large enough to eat a fucking full grown tiger latched onto one of his wings. Thrynn's pained roar ripped to her as he fell -

"No!"

Seeing their chance the shadows moved, predators surrounding a wounded prey. His magic lifted alongside his sword but there were too many – he was falling -

"Thrynn!"

No fucking way.

Focusing her energy, she shot a bolt of light straight into the beast hanging from his wing – hoping like hell it could burn. It was a lucky hit – she'd never done something like that before – but it was enough. Thrynn ripped free, turning to lunge his blade through the beast's gaping maw.

His magic pulsed, the shock wave forcing the beasts away, tossing them in all directions for an instant of peace as he looked for her.

He turned, frantically searching for her among the shadows. She could feel it in the bond. She called to him, casting her light toward him – shielding this time and he saw her.

He called to her, she couldn't hear him but her name rang clear through the bond. "I'm alright!"

But his eyes widened in horror.

Something smashed into her back. It threw her to the ground, fangs tearing through her shoulder. She cried out, her magic swirling up to pulse hard, forcing the creature from her spine, but one wicked tooth remained lodged in her flesh.

Through and through – that's what the movies called it. Inches of bone hung from either side of her as the shock of it finally hit.

Oh *shit.*

"Not her! She's mine!"

She heard the wild call but the creatures heard nothing. They swirled in and out of the shadows, their shape inconstant and strange. Only the teeth, only the eyes were consistent. What little control the man had once had, evidently lost to the madness of his own frustration.

Another leaped, aiming for her throat, but Rool appeared out of nowhere, wearing the Hungarian Horntail again, his scales slick with blood and goo, fire bursting from his throat to cleanse. He went insane, mini-dragon on shadow creature, and he tore the thing to gory shreds before her eyes.

She coughed, blood spraying from her lips to coat the flattened corn stalks and soil, ripped and shredded at their feet. Fucking hell... There should be pain – there should be burning and aching and terror – but she was numb. Weak. The absence was almost worse because it felt like an end, like a door slowly closing her off from the world - her family, her friends...

Thrynn.

Clutching the fang, she saw him. Roaring his rage at the

Hell beasts as his sword slashed through wind and rain, shadow and flesh alike. He was a force of nature - his energy burning hot as a wildfire, surrounded in a mist of steam and gore.

Yet chaos raged.

It didn't make sense. There was no end. Any direction had been lost to the frenzy, there was no point, no intent anymore. It was just fury.

And it wasn't getting any smaller.

She fell to her knees. Digging her fingers into the soil, she centered herself, casting her energy deep to touch the web of the barrier. If this was the end she would go, but she would go touching the one's she loved - even if only like this.

There.

Dandelion energy shot down, focusing on her - her Gran's soul gripping her own. A deep blue, steady and terrified - her father as he did his best to hold his ground in a battle he couldn't hope to fight himself. An instant later, lavender engulfed her - and the pain returned.

Crying out with it, Thrynn heard her. His fear tearing at the bond even as he turned back to her. "Open yourself to me!"

She heard him. She wasn't sure how... But she heard him.

Falling to her side, she gripped the fang. Out - she needed it out *now* – but the blood – she couldn't grip it -

"Now, Julia!" On a terrifying roar his magic engulfed him, stilling the chaos around him as the beasts fell back with a shriek. In the stillness his wings beat hard. "Now!"

He shot into the air above her, his sword held high like an avenging angel -

Hers.

The pain tore at her core - but it was a better pain, a healing pain.

The bond strained.

She could see the light of it now - it burned.

"Choose me, Julia!" Thrynn called to her even as he chucked himself into the storm. "As I choose you!"

Yes.

"Yes!" It sputtered, the blood choking her. Focusing on the bond, she opened herself peeling back layer after layer of protection until nothing lay between them but the bond and her fragile, tentative soul. "Yes!" She screamed it - casting all she was through the bond.

Thrynn lit with it, swirling high through the storm to hover above - the light of the moon at his back, the energy from the *Caol* at his feet. Power unlike any he'd known wrapped him, golden and purple, blue and yellow, the strength of family, of mate-hood...

Of love.

Nothing could stand against him now.

Lifting his sword to the stars he called to the gods, energy wrapping the blade until it screamed with all the force of the wickedness beneath him.

"This darkness you bring to me, turn back on you
One times three.
In honor and glory I banish thee, as I will...
So may it be."

The storm lifted, Shades and chaos wrapping behind him, engulfing blade and bone in it's fury. He spun his sword and, with all the weight of the gods on his side, slammed through to the heart of the storm, the center of all this distruction, all this pain -

A boy.

The strength of the blow carried them both to the ground, the soil buckling beneath the force of their impact. The boy choked, eyes wide and terrified on Thrynn's.

Confusion.

Horror.

Blood and spittle coughed from his lips and his trembling hands lifted to grip the hilt of the sword pinning him to the ground.

"Hunter!" Julia gasped, clawing her way to their side. Everything hurt, every breath cost her dearly, but she pulled herself to them regardless. "Oh, Hunter..."

The male choked, “I-” Blood spilled from his lips as his eyes flashed a wild violet...

There was only fear now.

Thrynn kept his grip firm on the blade.

Julia framed his face in her hands, tears trekking through the shit and grime coating her cheeks, “Shh... It’s alright. Fuck, Hunter... Mom!" Her eyes wild, Julia threw her panic to the wind, praying that she would hear her. "We’ll help you. It’s going to be fine. Mom!”

Thrynn’s jaw clenched but he held strong. There was tragedy here, yes.

But there was justice too.

Hunter was fading. His light, so tainted and consumed with madness it was almost unrecognizable. But for a moment, just this one last real moment, he was only Hunter. The boy that teased her, the quarterback that led Murkwood High to the championships, the carpenter, the son.

“I’m sorry,” He sighed it.

And then he stilled.

“Oh fuck...” Julia sobbed, clutching his head to her chest even as Thrynn cradled her, “Hunter...”

“We have to go,” Thrynn lifted her but she clung, “We have to go now, Julia.”

“Get Mom, she can save him. She can-”

Thrynn nodded to Rool even as he tucked her face into his chest. Her light was fading – fast. The Shade's venom had tainted her blood – it was a miracle she'd held on this long.

Rool's energy flared, the *Caol* opening at his back.

“No, don't-” Julia shoved at him, weakening fast. “Hunter...”

“It's done.”

Thrynn hushed her, pressing her cheek to his as the stars stretched and bent to bring them home.

~Chapter Twenty Three~

Home

November 3, 2021

"It's almost weird," Julia met Thrynn's eyes when he squeezed her hand before nodding back to the Murphy's farm, "Being back, I mean. After everything."

"Hm," Thrynn scanned the land.

It was no surprise his mate came from here.

Every place has a spirit, a name, a story to tell. Land like this, open and fresh, nurtured directly by the hands that love and protect it, it sang a beautiful song. The amber hills waved in the breeze like the ocean, the trees proudly stretched to the clouds. Even so late in autumn, as everything began to quiet and fade into slumber for the winter, it was beautiful.

And the farm house blended right in. Two stories tall and charmingly weathered by wind and rain, the windows glowed even through the gossamer curtains that sent them sparkling.

"It suits you," He said slowly and Julia's smile softened.

"It's home."

Home.

Thrynn thought of the endless empty corridors of Yvelta, all the memories and the quiet promise it held for him. How lovely would it be to see such warmth burn within once more? How satisfying and sweet to hear children laugh as they romped with reckless abandon through the halls. Free. Because it belonged to them. Safe. Because it stood for them and always would.

He longed for it.

And this family, these Murphys - they would be the beginning.

"Come on then."

Thrynn allowed Julia to tug at his hand until they finally reached the threshold. Before they could even knock, Gran threw the door open with all her typical enthusiasm, "There you are! By the gods, Boyo, took you long enough. What were you looking at, the gutters? I've been telling Eric to get on them for weeks now – all set to grow a forest up there, I swear - but-"

"Hey there, Gran. So wonderful to see you. Me? I'm just dandy, thanks. Still a bit sore after, you know, getting stabbed by a terrifying shadow monster that controlled lightening and wanted to do all manner of wicked things to my body, but-"

"Julia," Her dad warned but she heard the laughter in the word, "Be nice to your Gran. You know she's a bit dotty in her old age."

"Dotty!" Gran blustered, "Dotty, my ass! How dare you-"

"Baby!" Ever the gentle and elegant of the bunch, JoAnna rounded the corner fast as a bullet to wrap her arms around her little girl and squeeze. "You're back!" She cradled her little girl's face in her hands and let the tears fall, "Oh thank god..." She murmured it, her voice thick. "You were gone- Just... I felt your wound and then – You were gone."

"I'm here, Mama." Because they both needed it, Julia clung just as hard, "I'm alright."

It almost made him feel bad for taking Julia to Yvelta to recover.

Almost.

Thrynn stiffened in surprise when JoAnna rounded on him, wrapping her arms around his neck and encompassing him in a flurry of warmth and lavender.

"Thank you, Cern, for bringing her home to me." Leaning back she cupped his face, quiet tears spilling from her eyes, "You've no idea the gift you give us."

"Oh, I don't know about that." Gran sent him a wicked wink, "Our girl's been claimed right and ready if I've ever seen it-"

"Seen what?" Eric narrowed his eyes on the two of them as though squinting would make something appear.

"The bond, you dolt!" Gran waved at them, "You can see it all over their faces even if you can't see the thing shining between them like the damn sun."

Julia cleared her throat, "Uh, about that."

But JoAnna was already waving her away, "No need to explain. I saw it the moment I saw him in the apartment the other day-"

"You did?" Gran blustered all over again, "How in hell did you-"

"Gifted empath, indeed," Thrynn murmured and lifted JoAnna's fingers to buss a chaste kiss over her knuckles, "And you didn't say anything?"

"Nature must take her course - even if I don't always understand or approve."

Eric gripped Julia, pulling her into his arms for a quick embrace and, if he were honest, to reassure himself that he still could. It wasn't that he'd never prepared himself for this – he'd just always assumed he'd have to walk her down the isle in the usual way.

Gran beat him to it, "You'd better still be planning to marry our girl all official like. Don't be letting her live in sin and all that."

"Gran, for the love of god, this is the twenty-first century." Julia rolled her eyes but Thrynn didn't miss the spark of hope there.

He sent her a gentle smile and, though he didn't touch her, he opened the bond to show her the love he felt here, for her, in this home. "Aye," He murmured, "If she'll have me."

"Really?" Julia hadn't expected that. Hell, what they already shared was beyond anything a legal document could do - but she couldn't deny how much she'd wanted the tradition. The sharing of it. The memory. The vows before the gods and all their friends and family. "You'd do that?"

"Claim you? Over and over again, Sweetheart. Let all the beings in every realm hear tell of the day Thrynn, Lord of the Wild Things, Master of Yvelta, Son and heir of Gwynterra and Xyria was accepted by his fated mate. There would be nothing but joy in it, my Julia. I am proud to call you mine."

"Thrynn..." Eric stalled, "You're name's Thrynn? What the hell happened to not being able to lie?"

"He didn't lie," JoAnna smirked a little, "Not really." To calm him, she slipped into her husbands arms. "Cernunnos was a name our ancestors gave to him. He just went along when I suggested it, didn't you?"

Thrynn nodded slowly, "It's a name I was once called long ago." But still he thumped his chest and bowed just slightly before Eric, "'Twas not meant as a deception, I swear to it. It's a dangerous thing-"

But Eric turned on his daughter, "Did you know? I mean, did he at least tell *you* the truth?"

Julia laughed a little though she did flush, "Yes! Yeah. God, Dad. We weren't lying to you, I swear! It's just that-"

"When you know of a Fae's true name, they can be compelled by you." A wicked sparkle flashed in Gran's eye even as her dandelion power flared around her. "Thrynn, Lord of the Wild Things, Master of Yvelta, Son and Heir of... Cripes I don't remember... I compel you."

Thrynn did his best not to wince even as he felt the brief magic bind him, instead he just lifted a regal brow, "Well?"

They couldn't know how insulting this was - how infuriating. This was his mate's family - he made her happy, it was evident in all that she was. There was no way they would do something foolish and cruel like attempt to force him away from her... Would they?

"You will speak the truth – the simple truth." For once all humor was gone from Gran as she stared him down. The moment was somber, and heavy. "What are your intentions towards our Julia?"

Everything softened.

Thrynn smiled, his eyes warming with his magic as it reached out to touch each member of her clan, all those who awaited his answer so eagerly. He wanted them to feel his honesty. He wanted them to know.

"She will be my queen. Mistress of Yvelta. She will travel the realms at my side, learning and growing into the mage she was always meant to become." His eyes met hers flashing, "She will be the mother of my children. The one and only being in the universe that holds my heart in her hands. And..."

He paused, taking the time to meet each of their gazes in turn.

"She will have her family at her side, as long as she wishes it. I will do all in my power to keep her safe and make her happy every day of our lives. And should nature claim her? I will follow close behind.

Our souls are one... This I vow."

A beat of silence. It resonated between them all, but Thrynn watched his mate – her eyes shining.

Julia raced into his arms and he caught her readily. Gods, but he was so ready for her, for them, for the life they would build together.

"I love you." She cupped his face, bringing her brow to his, "Gods, I love you."

Enraptured, he kissed her. Thoughtless of the family ranged around them he dominated her, pouring every ounce of the gratitude and hope he felt through the bond, basking in hers as she rose to meet him. "I love you too, *mo chroi.*"

"You'd better still be planning to marry her-" JoAnna started.

But Gran only cackled and slapped her daughter on the shoulder, "Hell, that was better than any marriage vows I've ever heard."

Eric cleared his throat, loudly. Really now, there was only so much a man could take. And after sprinting through the carnage all those days ago to find his best friend's only son dead and his daughter missing... Everything just needed to slow the Hell down for a bit. "Let's at least take this to the living room, alright? I'd like to sit down if I'm going to have to suffer another heart attack."

Gran cackled and she sent him a twinkling wink, "Feels shit, doesn't it. Imagine how I felt hearing my young one had gone and given her heart to a farmer... An American at that."

JoAnna rolled her eyes, "As though America and the Otherworld are one and the same..." She muttered but Eric just wrapped an arm around her shoulders to squeeze.

"Doesn't look like she's complaining," So he kissed her soundly. "Still though," He nodded everyone through to the overstuffed couches where they could relax near the fire, "I've got questions."

"Me too," Julia bit her lip.

Gran hopped in, "Let's start with this one: How in all Hell did that Thompson boy do the things he did?"

JoAnna cocked her head, "I've wondered that too. I didn't know the boy personally all that well, but I've been around him plenty since he was just little. His daddy is one of our oldest friends. I would know if they had Fae blood, I'm sure of it."

"A dormant line?" Eric asked but Thrynn was shaking his head.

"Nay," He settled beside Julia, tucking her into his chest. It had taken days for her wounds to heal, even at Yvelta, even with all his power. The venom of those beasts was a brutal insidious kind meant to kill the strongest of Otherkin and it had wreaked havoc on her Human vessel. They'd come close – far too close – to losing her, and the thought still made him sweat. "No offspring of a dormant line could have done the things he did."

"What then?" Julia paled a little at Thrynn's expression but it wasn't him that spoke.

"Changeling," Gran breathed. A mixture of shock and horror dulling her usual glow.

"That's impossible," JoAnna scoffed but she didn't sound sure, not of anything anymore. "We were there the day Hunter was born – we babysat his sisters while Helena gave birth, remember?"

Thrynn sighed, "Tell me, JoAnna. When the Thompson's birthed their boy, were there... Complications?"

"Miracle baby," Eric murmured.

JoAnna gasped, "That's right. Hunter's heart, it was weak. It failed during delivery but when they set him aside to be swaddled before tending to Helena, he woke. They kept him in NICU for weeks trying to figure it out, but the doctor's could never explain it. He was healthy and strong-"

"It's not a common practice," Thrynn murmured, "Not anymore. But Hunter... Even for an Otherkin he displayed a level of power virtually unheard of – especially as he lacked any formal guidance."

"But why?" Julia nudged him, "Why would any Fae leave their child here?"

Thrynn's jaw clenched, "Do you remember how my family fell?"

Julia softened, to soothe him she laid her palm over his, warmth and sweetness coating the bond, "Yes."

"That war. It wasn't brief. It happened centuries ago for your people, and it spanned decades. The Otherworld... It's vital to all creation it bridges that it remain balanced, that it's heart remain healthy. When villages burned and entire people's were displaced... It was considered a gift to bring the child to another realm, giving them to a family who would have lost their own so that they may be raised with love. It was never meant to be a permanent solution, the child should have been collected for training when they reached maturity, but with my realm in chaos such things may well have been neglected."

"But then..." Eric scrubbed at his face – like father like daughter, "Whose was he?"

Thrynn winced, this was the part he hadn't wanted to say. To share it, perhaps he feared it would make it true. It would mean he'd failed. Somewhere, somehow along the line his enemy had breached his borders... "The Usurper King, no one realized how far he was willing to go to win the crown.

He created creatures – soulless creatures, mindless predators of shadow and soil-"

"The beasts?"

"Aye," He soothed Julia when he felt her jolt of fear, "The *Gan Anam.*"

"Soulless," Gran breathed.

"Shades. They made up his primary army. They threw the realm into chaos as they fed constantly but gave nothing in return. They were of him – crafted by him – and only he could control them."

"But Hunter-"

"I'm sorry," Thrynn brushed a wayward strand behind Julia's ear, "I told you that I defended this realm. I thought I had."

"Are you saying he's the King?"

"No," JoAnna brought trembling fingers to her lips, if they were right, if this were true... This darkness had only been the beginning. Child's play.

"He was his son."

About The Author

Ashlyn Grace

Ashlyn Grace graduated with a BA in English from Cottey College, and is now living with her husband Jon, their rambunctious three year old son, blue heeler and two judgemental cats in rural Oklahoma.

Books By This Author

Marked: Ancestral Wars Book One

"If you didn't have bad luck, you'd have no luck at all."

I doubt my dad meant those words to be even half as prophetic as they turned out to be but alas, here we are. Tucked in the arm-pit of the Adrienic where anti-human sentiments were practically legendary in their cruelty, the High Council's announcement couldn't have come at a worse time. The Marked had awakened, the champion of the Human race was out there somewhere just waiting to fulfill the prophecy and claim their throne and here I am, a Clanless Human sporting a funky birthmark on my forearm and a bad attitude.

I never would have guessed what it could mean.

But it's hard to argue with the King of the Isles, especially when he shows off his own birthmark, the mirror image of my own. Now he's talking about mates and coups, and I've got a strange new magic that I have to figure out how to control before the High Council and their loyalists show up to wipe us off the map.

Lucky?

Hell, I'm just hoping I don't blow myself up before I can figure out how to save my family.

www.ingramcontent.com/pod-product-compliance
Lightning Source LLC
LaVergne TN
LVHW012051160826
845678LV00014B/2781

* 9 7 9 8 7 5 5 8 0 3 9 7 7 *